Base to McCormick. McCormick, come in! Retreat! Retreat!

Even disguised in his commanding officer's voice, the warning signals firing off in Travis's head couldn't get through the static of full-blown desire that was short-circuiting every common-sense impulse in his body.

This girl was a natural. Every move he made, she answered back with her lips and a chorus of hot, sexy moans that hummed in her throat. He wanted her closer and she'd obliged. No, she'd taken charge with innocent abandon, crawling on top of him, spreading her knees beside his hips, rubbing her breasts against his chest and sinking that white promise of satisfaction against his throbbing groin.

He dragged his lips to her throat to taste the drumming beat of her pulse beneath his tongue. "Trav—" she gasped, arching her back and inviting his lips into the unbuttoned gap of her shirt.

Retreat, soldier! Retreat!

But his mind was lost in the moment – lost in his reawakening sense of power, of virility. He was lost in a woman – his old friend, Tess. And he suddenly knew his life would never be the same again...

Dear Reader,

As my brother headed into a war zone for the second time in his life, I found it difficult to get started on this story with a wounded military hero the way I'd originally envisioned it. But after some introspection (and good talks with my family and the families of other military personnel – you guys rock!), I decided the focus wouldn't be on the thrills and dangers inherent in such a career – though that still plays a key role in the story – but rather on the joys and challenges of coming home after being in the action.

Many military spouses, parents, siblings and children I spoke with talked about how some things never change when a loved one is away, serving his or her country, while other things change greatly. Expectations must be flexible, and often family members and service personnel must adapt to new roles while apart, and again when reunited.

Dealing with such changes became the focus of *Basic Training*. Tess and Travis have returned to the town where they grew up – and on the surface, it seems like old home, old friends, old times. But they soon realise that she's no longer just the girl-next-door, and her Marine Corps hero is more than the hunky best friend he used to be.

I hope that readers can feel the happiness, pride and relief of family, friends and community welcoming home one of their own. I also hope you'll enjoy the journey as Tess and Travis evolve into their new roles – deeper, bolder, sexier and closer than two friends have a right to be.

Happy reading,

Julie Miller

BASIC TRAINING

BY
JULIE MILLER

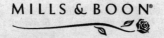

MILLS & BOON®

For the 110th Engineer Battalion. Prayers and
pride for those soldiers and their families.
And for my favourite Captain in particular,
be smart, watch your back and take care. Love you.

*First published in Great Britain 2007
by Harlequin Mills & Boon Limited, Eton House,
18-24 Paradise Road,
Richmond, Surrey TW9 1SR*

© Julie Miller 2006

ISBN: 978 0 263 85570 8

14-0407

*Printed and bound in Spain
by Litografía Rosés S.A., Barcelona*

1

TRAVIS MCCORMICK had come home.

"Travis," Tess Bartlett whispered. She tucked her suitcase into the closet of her old bedroom and hurried to the window to see with her own eyes the return of the conquering hero.

He'd come so far. Been through so much.

Tess was almost ashamed to admit that she'd barely ventured away from the homefront. After college, one thing after another had seemed to draw her back to Ashton, Virginia. She'd come home when a cancer scare had left her widowed mother feeling vulnerable and alone. Then, she'd done her physical therapy internship here and stayed on when the hospital had offered her a generous salary to become a member of their staff.

She had her own apartment, her own career. She had old and new friends who were an integral part of her life. And when push came to shove, she could even finagle herself a date on a Saturday night.

But in one way, Tess had never moved on. Tess had never shared a bond with anyone, not even her sister and mother, like the one she shared with Travis. She'd lived so much of her life vicariously through him. He was a military hero with skills and knowledge she could only guess at. As a Marine, he'd traveled the world. Fought beside the bravest warriors and strategized with the best military minds.

And yet she'd always, always believed he was glad to come back to Ashton to see her, his little buddy Tess.

Over the years of their friendship, he'd confessed triumphs and tribulations that were their secrets alone. He never hesitated to offer a hug or a wink or a smile. He'd stood beside her and taken the heat when their youthful practical jokes had gotten them into trouble. And she'd stood beside him and listened and held his hand when that strong United States Marine hadn't been quite strong enough.

Would their friendship take up where they'd left off before he'd been called up for a covert assignment more than a year ago? She was thrilled that he was finally coming home to Ashton after spending most of that year in a hospital and therapy. But she knew he wouldn't be thrilled that he'd been injured while training for that mission—before ever shipping out overseas.

Despite the circumstances, was he looking forward to reconnecting with an old friend for a few weeks as much as she was?

Hidden by the glare of the afternoon sun off the water from Chesapeake Bay, Tess peeked through the curtains of the second-story bedroom window in the house where she'd grown up, next door to the McCormicks' bayside colonial. She and her older sister, Amy, had timed their annual summer get-together with their mom to coincide with the U.S. Marine Corps captain's home-coming. They were all invited over that evening for a welcome-home party, but Tess couldn't wait that long to see him with her own eyes. She couldn't wait to reassure herself that the boy next door—her classmate, teammate, and longtime friend—had finally come home after a full year.

She was thirty-three years old, had known Travis for more than half her life, and she still couldn't stop that little hitch in her breath each time she saw him. Damn the man. He was that good looking. Each reunion stirred her blood—as if she were discovering that well-sculpted hunk of testosterone for the first time. Discovering those clear blue eyes, that sexy crop of dark blond hair hugging the perfect shape of his head, and those shoulders broad enough to lead men and seduce women with equal success.

Tess closed her eyes and diligently ignored the heated rush of hormones that tripped along her pulse. She and Travis had been friends for far too long. She knew his taste in women—everything from busty and mysterious to slim and flirty. Blondes, brunettes, redheads all qualified—just as long as they weren't afraid of their sexuality, and weren't hung up about the whole commitment thing.

Tess opened her eyes on a frustrated huff. She might as well enjoy the view because that's all she'd be getting. No way in hell did she qualify as more than a friend to Travis. They'd shared just that one awkward kiss in college—and fortunately, Travis had been too drunk to remember it. Her inability to turn his head was probably why they'd been able to remain such good friends over the years.

First, the word *sexy* simply didn't apply to her practically-proportioned body, which was better suited for softball than seduction. Her bland hazel eyes and generic brown hair had never turned heads. Even with contact lenses to halt the nickname of "Four Eyes" from high school, and a few golden highlights to give her ponytail some pizzazz, she still oozed smarts and sensibility—not sex appeal.

Second, her sense of humor and reliability, which made her a trusted ally when it came to pulling off practical jokes and keeping secrets, made her a dud in the come-hither department. Back in high school she'd learned that sweaty shortstops and salutatorians didn't get asked to the senior prom if they lacked the boobs or legs or feminine mystique to compensate for an error-free season and nearly perfect GPA.

And third, in a small town like Ashton, Virginia, once you got labeled with a reputation for being a brainiac or tomboy or good ol' gal, you were stuck.

Tess had been stuck for fifteen years.

"Hey, Tess. You upstairs?" Ah, yes. Her big sister, Amy, had much nicer labels. She had managed to get the right blend of genes to allow her to be smart, accomplished *and* sexy. Of course, she also wound up with the gene that allowed her to marry a real loser, and now the newly divorced school teacher had returned to her roots as much to heal from the nasty breakup as to support the Bartlett women's summer tradition of helping out at the festival. "Tess?"

Tess drew back from the window as if the call might alert the McCormicks to her subtle spying. "In here."

But she couldn't walk away. Not until she saw for her own eyes that Travis was alive. That the bomb that had shredded his body hadn't killed him. That his handsome mouth could still smile and those devilish blue eyes could still sparkle with mischief.

Tess answered the soft knock at her door without turning away from the scene visible through the lacy sheers at her window. "Come on in."

"Getting a sneak peek before tonight's festivities?" Amy asked, curling her long legs beneath her as she perched on the corner of Tess's bed.

"I'm just anxious to see Trav," Tess admitted, watching Travis's father, retired Brigadier General Hal McCormick, climb out from behind the wheel of his silver Chevy Suburban and stride up the sidewalk to the front door. Even at age 60, with a dusting of silver in his short blond hair, the man's military bearing was unmistakable. "The last time I talked to Travis in the hospital, he told me not to come visit. Said he'd be home soon enough."

Amy frowned as she joined Tess at the window. "What was that—two, three months ago?"

"Try six." She hugged her arms around her waist, trying not to feel the lingering sting of his rejection. "He's been out of the hospital since then, but I doubt he'd be in Ashton now if he hadn't finally been ordered to take some R and R. Hal said he'd been working a desk job, but that Travis was so gung-ho about getting back to his Special Forces unit and whatever mission they were prepping for that he overdid his physical training and actually set back his recovery."

A pretty, perky brunette Tess identified as Travis's sister-in-law, J.C., climbed out of the backseat and opened the back of the Suburban to retrieve a couple of suitcases. J.C.'s husband, Ethan McCormick, followed right behind her in his khaki and olive green lieutenant colonel's uniform. He took both suitcases from her. She snatched one back. The argument that flared briefly between them ended with a perfunctory kiss. And then another, lingering this time. Then one more that lasted long enough for Amy and Tess to sigh in unison.

"You know, I always thought that at least one of us would wind up with a McCormick." Amy crossed her arms to match Tess's stance. They both giggled as Ethan's independent wife let him have the suitcase he insisted on carrying, but then pulled another bag from the car and scooted around him to follow Hal before Ethan could stop her. "We've lived next door to those two hotties for how many years? Now I'm divorced from Barry Can't-Keep-His-Pants-Zipped, and you're . . ."

Doomed to spinsterhood? Sentenced to celibacy?

Amy pursed her lips, searching for the right word to finish her sentence. "Unattached." Her brown eyes were full of honest regret as she looked down at Tess. "You know I don't mean anything by that, right? You could have any man you wanted if you stopped listening to what the busybodies in this town have to say and just set your mind to it. Mom said you'd been dating Morty Camden," she added hopefully.

"Sure. Rub salt in an old wound. Morty might be the one person in town who's getting less sex than I am."

Her big sister didn't seem entirely relieved that Tess had made a joke of it. "But sex isn't the only reason to go out with a guy, right? He's a nice guy, isn't he? Doesn't he run his own business?"

"He's nice enough," Tess agreed. She was having a hard time picturing Morty's earnest face and receding hairline as she waited for Travis to emerge from the vehicle below them. "He has his own accounting firm.

But he's just a friend. Basically, we're each other's escort whenever something comes up."

They served together on the same committee that organized the fishing competition and other events for Ashton's annual Summer Bay Festival. Slated to start the following Monday and run the first full week of July, the festival drew in tourists, locals and a slew of sailors, Marines and soldiers from nearby bases for a celebration both on and off the water of Chesapeake Bay. Her "dates" with Morty had been little more than friendly business meetings. The closest they'd come to bodily contact was a little hand holding and a few high-five's.

But Tess didn't elaborate. Ethan had closed the rear hatch and was circling the car now. Leaning forward ever so slightly, Tess peered through the slit in the curtains. "Don't you think there's something a little too big-brotherly about Ethan and Travis for us to get involved with either of them?"

Man, she wished she believed what she'd said. But she'd lusted after Travis for too many years. And that one collegiate kiss had confirmed that *brotherly* wasn't really the way she felt about him. But it was the way she *had* to feel. He was her best bud. And since he'd never see her in any other way—not while sober, at any rate—

"I don't know. I dated Ethan that summer after high school—before he took off for Annapolis." Amy's husky sigh left Tess wondering just how far those dates had gone, and whether she was the only Bartlett with lust in her heart.

"Did you and Ethan ever do it?"

"Tess!" Amy's flawless skin darkened with a rosy blush.

Tess pointed an accusatory finger, but she was laughing. "Tell me."

Her sister tucked her thick, honey blond hair behind her ears and bought some time before she answered. "Even back then, Ethan was all about being a Marine. As sweet and smart as he was, he was saving himself for the Corps. I don't think he would have jumped my bones even if I had USS *Amy* tattooed on my boobs."

Tess narrowed her gaze. She wasn't getting the whole story. "But you blushed. You're holding back."

Amy arched a golden eyebrow in that mystery-woman expression that men found so irresistible. Tess had tried to duplicate the same maneuver for years, but could only manage to arch both brows at once and come off looking more like Larry, Curly and Moe than any femme fatale. "We never went all the way. Let's just say, he scouted out the ship."

"You rat. So... how was he? Is Ethan a good kisser?" Maybe it was a family trait.

Amy's wistful smile gave the answer before she spoke. "J.C.'s a lucky bride. And not just because he's such a stand-up guy."

"So, are you okay with Ethan marrying someone else? Do you wish things had been different?"

"You mean do I wish I'd married Ethan instead of Barry?" Her resolute sigh spoke volumes. "It wasn't in the cards for Ethan and me. The chemistry just wasn't there—not like it is with J.C. Even at eighteen, we were smart enough to know we made better friends than we'd make lovers. On the other hand, I had chemistry up the wazoo with Barry. Sex was always great with him. Of course, apparently, it was also great with all the other women in his life." She hugged her arms around her own waist as she shared a painful nugget of hard-won wisdom. "I needed Barry to be a better friend."

Tess had already suspected as much. "So you're saying that you can't mix the two—that a man can't be a great friend and a great lover?"

"It's been impossible for me."

Maybe Tess held her sister's gaze a moment too long and gave something away. By the time she'd turned back to the window to spy on Travis, Amy was wrapping an arm around her shoulders.

"That was *my* experience, kiddo. I'm sure it's different for other men and women."

Not for her. Tess had more male friends than she could count. She hadn't had a lover since…oh, crap… had it really been three summers ago? A forgettable one-night stand with a visiting soldier she'd met in a bar during the Bay Festival. Yikes. How trite.

At that time, she'd been thinking way too much about Travis's kiss and wondering why no other man's passion had ever equalled that one, perfect, stupid night. Maybe over the years, she'd idealized what had almost happened between them. So instead of wallowing in what-if's and why-not's, she'd thrown caution to the wind and jumped into bed with the eager soldier. Ugh. So much for life on the wild side. She hadn't seen any action since.

Big sis gave Tess a stern shake. "Hey. The right man is out there for you—one who can flip your switch and you still trust him in the morning." She peeked out the window. "Who knows? Maybe he's right under your nose."

Tess scoffed. "Travis?"

"Why not?" Amy shrugged. "Since I'm currently off men at the moment, and Ethan went and found his own woman, that means it's up to you and Travis to finally bring the Bartletts and McCormicks together."

"Yeah, right. You just said men and women can't be friends *and* lovers." Tess managed to smile. "Hal hired me to be Travis's physical therapist while he's at home. I'm not his dating service. I'm sure once the ladies of Ashton hear that the 'Action Man' is back in town, they'll be lining up with chicken soup and skimpy negligees, ready to fulfill his every need."

Amy reprimanded her little sister with stern brown eyes. "Hey. Don't sell yourself short. I'll bet Travis or Morty or a dozen other men in this town would love to see you in a skimpy negligee."

"Two problems with that scenario," Tess insisted. "One, I don't own anything skimpy, and two—"

But she never got to the joke about how she knew more about making chicken soup than seducing a man.

Instead, she pulled the curtain aside and held her breath as Travis unfolded himself from the backseat of his father's car—with Ethan's help. She frowned as the green camouflage uniform stiffly straightened itself to take the shape and form of the man whom she'd always cared so deeply about.

Travis was a leaner, harder version of his more muscular brother. The athleticism that had fine-tuned his body for battle was still evident, but his balance was off. Travis hauled himself up by the car frame, plopped a cloth cap over his short, burnished hair. Then he held on to Ethan's arm while he retrieved something from the backseat.

A cane.

"Poor Travis," Amy whispered in sympathy. "I had no idea."

Tess's hand fisted around the edge of the curtain, betraying the concern and compassion that gripped her chest just as tightly.

Once he was free of the car door, Travis shook Ethan off and proceeded up the driveway to the front door under his own power. But Tess's sharp eye for physical weaknesses and pain could tell that, despite the unwavering set of his shoulders, Travis was relying heavily on that cane. His left leg was stiff—probably from the long drive from the Quantico military base near Washington, D.C. And she suspected that if he didn't have the hardheaded determination of the Corps drilled into him, he'd be limping.

That perfect body had taken a few more hits than she'd been led to believe.

He wasn't even smiling.

Whether playing a joke, flirting with a woman, or striking out a batter, Travis McCormick almost always smiled.

Splaying her fingers against the glass at her window, cool from the air-conditioning, Tess reached out to her friend. Ashton's hometown hero had come home, all right. But he hadn't made it in one piece.

"Trav," she whispered, her warm breath close enough to fog the glass.

Travis paused on the front sidewalk, almost as if he'd heard her soft plea.

By the time he turned and looked up, Tess had swiped the pane clear and ducked away from the window, letting the curtain fall back into place. Somehow, it seemed wrong to be spying on her childhood friend and longtime hero when he wasn't feeling up to snuff. He'd always been so strong. So sure of himself. So perfect.

Tess retreated another step, pulling Amy with her toward the center of the room. "Did you come up here for a reason?"

She had to change to subject, focus her mind on something else, before she ran downstairs and across the yard to see Travis face to face. To hug him, touch him, ensure with her own two hands that his body hadn't been damaged beyond repair—and that the scars and weakened leg didn't mean that his fighting spirit and wicked charm had been wounded as well.

"Mom wanted your opinion on the cake she's baking for tonight. She said you'd know Travis's tastes better than either of us. Does he like chocolate? White?"

"Lemon." Travis had always had a taste for food with a little attitude. Just like his women. "He'd want a lemon cake."

At least the old Travis would. Now she was beginning to wonder how much of the old Travis still existed—and wonder how she could help heal this newer, harder, humbler version of the man who had always been her best friend.

"I'll tell her." If Amy had any inkling of the turmoil spinning inside Tess's head, the only sign was the teasing tug on her younger sister's ponytail. "Come on down when you're done unpacking. We could use your help before the party. Mom's fixing enough food to feed the entire town."

Tess nodded. "I'll be there in a sec."

By the time Amy left and Tess dared to return to the window, Travis had gone inside the house with his brother.

She'd been patient for twelve long months, ever since she'd first gotten the news that he'd nearly died in that accident.

He was hurt. He was her responsibility as his therapist. He was her *friend*.

Screw waiting until tonight.

Tess tucked her T-shirt into her denim shorts and dashed down the stairs.

"Tessa, I need… Where is that girl going?"

"Give her a few minutes, Mom."

Her mother's and sister's voices were cut off by the noise of the screen door slamming behind her. Tess jogged across the lawn separating the two houses, and tucked a few stray waves into her ponytail as she slowed to a walk to climb the steps to the McCormicks' front porch. She knocked, then fixed a grin on her face as Hal McCormick answered the door.

The older gentleman's welcoming smile reminded her of her late father, who had died the same year Hal had lost his wife to cancer.

"Hey, Hal."

"Tess Bartlett. Come here." He scooped her up in a bear hug and set her down inside the tiled foyer of his home. "Is it girls' week at the Bartletts' again? I swear, Tess, you look prettier every time I see you."

She waved aside the compliment. "And you're more full of the blarney every time I see you. Did you have a good trip?"

He shrugged. "As good as could be expected. You and your family are coming tonight, right?"

"We'll be here." She let her gaze scan up the stairs to the second floor where Travis's old bedroom was located. Surely, with his injured leg, they'd prepared a room downstairs for him. But she didn't see anyone else moving about. "I know I'm early. And I promise I won't stay long. But I saw the car and wanted to welcome Travis home. I'll give him a hug, then get out of your hair so you guys can rest up."

"He went to the guest room, and I don't—"

A king-size belch, starting deep and covering a variety of pitches, dramatic in its longevity and loud enough to tickle her funny bone, erupted from the back of the house. An instant later, Travis material-ized in the archway leading to the kitchen, holding a can of soda.

Tess grinned and gave him a thumbs-up. "Nice one."

Clear blue eyes swallowed up her seeking gaze from across the room. "I've been practicing."

"Travis Harold McCormick. There's a lady in the house."

She'd never envied Travis and Ethan for getting the double whammy of a superior officer's tone and a father's voice rolled into one. But the McCormick boys didn't seem to mind.

"It's cool, Dad. It's just Tess." He downed the last of the soda and reached around the archway frame to set the can on a counter. "Hey, T-bone."

Tess shook her head at the goofy nickname, but her eyes never wavered as she studied him from head to toe. The killer smile was still there, bemused and sexy, even if it looked a little ragged around the edges. But there were other subtle changes. There was a gauntness to his chiseled features that hadn't been there before, a tension, a maturity. And a wash of pale beneath his golden tan indicated that the deepening web of lines beside his eyes had more to do with stress and fatigue than with time spent outdoors.

"Keep it short, son. The doctor said you need to get off that leg as soon as possible." He held up a stern, paternal finger. "And mind your manners."

"I'll make sure he follows orders, General." Tess smiled with reassurance.

Hal gave her a wink, then excused himself from the foyer.

"Good to see you." Travis had tossed his hat onto the living room couch beside his cane, and with a nonchalant defiance, he closed the distance between them. The stiff set of his jaw told her what it was costing him to hide his limp without the aid of his cane.

Tess hurried to meet him halfway.

"It's good to see you, too." Her words caught in a strangled whisper as she fought the sudden tears burning in her throat. "Welcome home, Captain."

She reached up to touch the tight lines of strain beside his mouth. She brushed her fingertips across the pale pink scars that lined the left side of his square jaw and dotted his neck. She caught his chin and turned it from side-to-side, inspecting every mark.

The eyes were as blue as she remembered, the nose the same sharp blade. The amusement on those firm, flat lips was genuine. "You just gonna stare?" he teased, spreading wide his welcoming arms. "Or am I gonna get some action?"

Exhaling a cry of relief, she rose up on tiptoe and

kissed his smooth, angular cheek. Then she threw her arms around his neck and squeezed him tight.

Riding the deep breath that filled his chest, Tess held on as Travis wrapped his arms behind her waist and lifted her off the floor. She squeezed her eyes shut and buried her nose in his collar. He smelled of soap and hospital and the starch in his uniform. Intoxicating. Worrisome. Strange yet familiar.

"Couldn't get a good enough look through your window?"

His teasing voice rumbled against her ear, and Tess was suddenly aware of how tightly they held each other. How distinctly non-platonic this felt. Her nipples beaded where her small breasts pillowed against the hard plane of his chest. Her cotton T-shirt and his canvas uniform couldn't mask the heat seeping from his skin into hers.

Or maybe she was the one whose body temperature had suddenly soared. "You saw me?"

He laughed out loud as she squirmed away, sliding down his body and creating a friction that sparked every nerve with an embarrassing hyperawareness.

Travis reached out and cupped her blushing cheek. "I saw the curtain move. I remembered all the times we sent messages back and forth between our upstairs bedroom windows and put two and two together. Nice to know you're still lookin' out for me."

"I'm going to be doing more than that, Trav." She retreated another step to gain some much-needed distance. "I'm in charge of your therapy while you're here."

The smile vanished. "Therapy? I'm on forced R and R."

"Your physical rehabilitation. Starting Monday." She shoved her hands into her pockets, wondering at the rapid cooldown in Travis's mood. "I'm a licensed therapist, remember? I work with sports injuries, accident victims, stroke patients, wounded veterans." She shifted back and forth on her feet. Travis was damn near glowering now. "You dad told you, didn't he? I've read the reports from your doctors and have outlined a recovery plan that should have you back to Quantico in four to six weeks' time. All we have to do is set up a schedule that's convenient for you."

A glimpse of the tough, six-foot, two-inch, Special Ops Marine surfaced as he leaned in. Leaned over her. All traces of the familiar camaraderie he'd greeted her with were gone.

"You'll be waiting by your phone a long, long time. I'm here for two weeks, tops," he insisted. "And if I wasn't concerned about the strain on Dad's heart from worrying about me, it'd be less than that."

Tess stood there and gaped, absorbing his anger, wondering at its cause. She curled her hands into fists at her side, unsure whether she wanted to slap him or hug him at his outburst, but knowing neither touch would help right now. "Look, Captain, I was only trying to help give you what you need."

"I know what I need—and it's not being stuck down here in Podunkville for six weeks while the Corps forgets about me. So unless you've got some miracle up your sleeve that can get me back on the front lines with my unit, there isn't going to be any rehabilitation."

2

TESS BARTLETT had tits.

Theoretically, Travis had always known they were there. But he'd never really noticed. Not the way a guy noticed an attractive woman. His body hadn't cared before.

But there they were, small but scrumptious things, sitting high and proud, on the opposite side of his father's living room where Tess chatted with her mother, Margaret, and one of the matriarchs of the community, Nixa Newhaven. He was damn sure Miss Newhaven hadn't noticed the beaded tips outlined beneath the cling of Tess's lavender T-shirt. No doubt they were jutting out in protest of the air-conditioning that ran constantly in the summer heat as partygoers streamed in and out of the house.

But Travis noticed.

His body had been misfiring with overheated aftershocks of physical awareness ever since that hug this afternoon. He'd felt them then, pressed against him like… well, not like Tess.

Hell, yeah, he'd been glad to see her. The two of them had hugged before. Countless times. But this afternoon it was…well, not like Tess.

He'd been pleased at first to see her. Finally, someone

with whom he could drop the brave face and relax. He'd been on his best behavior at Quantico, not wanting to give his superiors any more reason to drum him out of the Corps. His father and brother were far too worried about his recovery, adding guilt onto the layers of frustration that already plagued him.

Maybe Hal could be content with retirement, spending half his time on his fishing boat, or camping in one of the ocean-view parks. But Travis had been bred and built for action and adventure. A dozen steel pins in his left leg weren't going to stop him from getting back to the job he loved so much.

Though they'd done a damn good job of it so far.

That was the truth that scared him the most. His injuries might be the one enemy he couldn't defeat. Captain Travis McCormick, leader of a Special Ops unit that was the Marine Corp's equivalent of a Navy SEALs team, wasn't used to feeling fear. He wasn't used to feeling like a member of the losing team.

That's probably what had made him so testy this afternoon. So quick to jump down Tess's throat when she mentioned physical therapy. Man, he needed to apologize for being such an ass. Instead of trading hello's and falling into their comfortable routine, he'd dumped on her. No wonder she'd found a way to stay on her side of the living room all evening long.

But he couldn't afford four to six weeks of R and R at home, squeezing a rubber ball between his knees and lifting weights. He had to get back to his unit. They'd already assigned a new commander, but there was a chance he could still rejoin the team. They'd be stateside within the month, home to regroup, retrain and refit the team for a new assignment. He had to be there to join them. He had to prove he still had what it took to get the job done. Or else he'd be stuck serving out the remainder of his military career pushing papers—or worse, he'd be drummed out on an honorable discharge because he just couldn't cut it as a Marine anymore.

Yeah, that's all this crazy notion about Tess was. That was T-bone standing over there, making nice with her mom's friends—not some sexy woman he was itchin' to get his hands on. With his future in limbo, he just wasn't feeling right in his own skin, so his perception of things was way off.

He closed his eyes and tried to picture her in her softball uniform, complete with sweat-stained visor and clunky cleats. He remembered the first day he'd met her, a gawky fourteen year-old, ankle deep in mud with her wavy brown hair flying in all directions, crabbing in the slough at the end of the street.

Travis opened his eyes and glanced across the room.

Nope. They were still there. And she had a mighty fine pair of 'em from where he was standing.

Correction. From where he was sitting on the sofa, being waited on hand and foot like some damn invalid. It seemed as if most of Ashton's nontourist population had filed through his father's front door to shake his hand or kiss his cheek and wish him well as they welcomed him home. Every woman over the age of eighteen, it seemed, had brought some kind of food to tempt him with. Every man, it seemed, had some sort of anecdote to tell about his own service experience. Travis had a beer, an iced tea and a frosty lemonade all within his reach, and enough plates of food to feed his entire platoon. He could quote stories from Omaha Beach to Grenada to Iraq.

But neither the tiring hoopla nor his worries about his military career could completely distract him from his recent discovery.

Damn. Travis shifted uncomfortably in his seat and reached for the beer beside him. He drank two long, cold swallows and forced his attention back to Morty Camden, who didn't have a war story to share, but who had an apparent fascination with statistics and the numbers of troops from nearby bases at Norfolk, Newport News and Camp Pendleton he expected to flood the town for the Summer Bay Festival.

Travis dutifully listened to the amount of money that would pour into the town coffers next week. But if Tess Bartlett didn't stop propping her hand on her hip and standing in a way that made those little marvels jut out like temptation itself, then certain parts of his anatomy were about to prove, despite the opinion of a dozen doctors and half that many months of rehabilitative therapy, that he was no invalid.

He took another drink.

She was the girl next door. The tomboy who'd saved the world right by his side in their imaginary neighborhood games as kids. The good buddy who'd gotten him through Physics and Calculus, and introduced him to the three best dates of his high-school and college years.

Tess Bartlett was one of the guys. Somebody he could drink a beer with and rag on the Redskins to. She'd sent those newsy letters when he'd been stationed overseas and held his hand when he'd finally gotten home to visit his mother's grave.

Tess Bartlett was every bit the buddy that his dad, his brother, and a handful of Marines he'd served with were.

So when the hell had she sprouted boobs?

Morty adjusted his plastic-framed glasses on his nose, reminding Travis that his attention had wandered again. "We hope that you'll be able to help us with one of the booths or competitions next week." Morty dropped a glance to where Travis's black boot was propped up on the coffee table. "If you're up to it, that is."

Travis tugged at the leg of his camo pants and rested the beer bottle between his thighs. Oh yeah, he was gettin' up to something, all right. And my, my, wasn't that an uncomfortable realization to make.

He should go over there and apologize to Tess, then hook up with one of the willing young ladies who'd come to the open house, and get this unhealthy fascination with Tess Bartlett out of his system.

"We'll see." He had nothing against Morty. Like Tess, they'd been classmates back in high school, even if his jock-centered path had rarely crossed with the nearsighted valedictorian's. Still, he didn't want to make any promises he couldn't keep. "I'm not sure how long I'm going to be in town."

"Well, at least we hope you stick around long enough to come down and have some fun." Morty stuck out his hand and Travis automatically shook it.

Surprised at the solid strength of Morty's grip, Travis shook hands a second time. Either Tess wasn't the only Ashton resident who'd gone through a few changes since he'd been gone, or he needed a mental evaluation to go along with the physical he'd flunked last week. "Thanks, man. Appreciate the invitation."

Morty nodded and pushed to his feet. "No problem. I know you've got lots of folks you want to spend some time with so I'll head on out. Welcome home."

"Thanks."

Using Morty's departure as a chance to effect his own escape, Travis braced his hand against the back of the couch. He lowered his foot to the floor and pushed himself to a standing position. A pathway cleared instantly, and the roomful of guests turned in his direction.

He'd have laughed at all the unwanted attention if he wasn't so busy gritting his teeth while his left leg adjusted to holding his weight, and the sharp shaft of pain eased to a dull ache.

"No show here, folks." He waved aside his father, brother, and a couple other offers of help. Standing at near attention, he fixed a trademark smile on his lips, reassuring everyone enough to return to their conversations. He made an excuse to be dismissed. "I'm just off to the latrine. I think I can manage that on my own."

Fresh air was the ticket. Night. Solitude.

But if locking himself inside the john was the only way to get some time to himself so he could get his head on straight, then that was exactly what he planned to do.

His careful stride took him past Tess, allowing him to eavesdrop on the plea coming from Nixa Newhaven's pruney lips. "It would only be for four hours on Monday evening."

Four hours sacrificed for Miss Newhaven and her dowager cronies? What a downer.

A kindred spirit of being forced into something unpleasant made Travis stop there and exchange a few words with his father regarding his sister, Caitlin, her husband, Sean, and how they were going to make Hal a grandpa in the next two weeks. He already knew the facts and was delighted he was about to become an uncle, but at the moment, Travis was only listening to the short list of prospective baby names because it gave him an excuse to linger close enough to hear Tess's response.

"I was hoping to check out the festival myself Monday night. Before things get too crazy." Her tone, while polite enough, lacked the conviction to talk Miss Newhaven out of anything. "Besides, I'm working three other nights at the concession stand already."

Nixa tutted between her teeth. "Do you have an escort to go with you?"

"You mean a date? Well, no, not yet. I thought Amy and I—"

"You girls can't go out by yourself." Nixa's silver hair bent closer to Tess's golden brown ponytail to whisper, "There'll be sailors in town."

Oh, the shock of it all! Travis twisted his lips to hide his grin. There'd be Marines and soldiers and civilians, too. And he'd bet good money that if any one of them was a little too forward with Tess, she could handle herself just fine.

Of course, she might be wanting one of them to be a little forward. Maybe a lot forward. Travis's grin slipped. He hadn't been home to Ashton for a year. Maybe he didn't know Tess as well as he thought he did anymore. Was she seeing someone now? Dating around? Just because he'd never thought of her in that way before didn't mean some other guy hadn't noticed what a sweet package she'd morphed into.

Was she looking to meet someone? Get married? Have a fling? A one-night stand? And why the hell should her love life—in whatever form it might exist— get him all curious and itchy inside his skin like this? It wasn't any of his business. She was a grown woman— She could sleep with anyone she damn well liked. As long as the man respected her. Made it good for her.

Hell. Why was it turning him inside out to think about Tess and sex in the same sentence?

No. Tess and sex with some man Travis didn't know. Some jerk who wasn't good enough for her.

"Miss Newhaven," Travis heard Tess pipe up, "I have a right to a social life."

"Of course, you do, dear." Nixa Newhaven was patting Tess's hand now. "But you've always been so good about helping out when you're needed. I don't know who else to ask."

A breath of cool-headed logic seeped in to calm the unsettling stab of emotion. Tess had said she was working three nights next week. Nixa Newhaven seemed to think she was available to work a few nights more. And the older woman had asked whether Tess had a date.

Tess was unattached. Safe. He'd gotten himself all worked up over nothing.

Travis shouldn't be breathing any easier, but he was.

He relaxed and savored his next swallow as Tess tried again. "Miss Newhaven—"

"I don't claim to understand all these modern mores that you young people follow. But I really could use your help. Doris Mead simply can't tolerate the heat the way she used to and I said I'd find a replacement to work her shift at the concession stand. Since you don't have any specific plans…"

Since there was no *date* currently in the picture, Travis should do the gallant thing and give Tess the excuse she needed to get out of the assignment by asking her out himself. Yeah. He could just step up, offer Nixa a bit of a flirty smile to knock her off her garters, then chime in with something like, "Sorry, she can't be bored to tears for four hours. Tess and I have plans—sharing a couple of carnival rides, strolling through the historic shops of Ashton's Main Street, sipping margaritas on the dock, and then maybe taking a sailboat out onto the water to do a little canoodling under the moonlight."

Sure, he could do that. An unexpected rightness seemed to lift his mood. Lord knew it wouldn't be the first time he'd offered his services to a damsel in distress. He turned to join their conversation. Nixa tipped her chin, waiting expectantly when he smiled down at her. It sounded like a perfect evening. It sounded…

Wrong with Tess.

He swung his startled gaze over to lock onto Tess's green-gold eyes, tilted up with curiosity. "Trav?"

Travis rubbed his knuckles along the newly healed skin at his jaw, frowning at the bitter taste in his mouth. He shouldn't be thinking about canoodling with Tess. Or kissing or hugging—or stripping off that lavender T-shirt and whatever sensible thing she wore underneath to get a firsthand look at those perky, provocative breasts in all their naked glory.

"I'm sorry," he finally ground out between clenched teeth. He turned away from plain, practical Tess and mustered a smile for Nixa. "I figured you'd be turning in early, and just wanted to say goodnight in case I missed you later."

"That's so considerate of you. Isn't it, Tess?"

"Yes."

Before he could hear what else either of them had to say, before the intuitive concern shining in Tess's eyes figured out his crazily inappropriate urges, Travis walked away.

No. He limped.

He wasn't in a position to rescue anybody—even from something as harmless as Nixa Newhaven's pushy assumptions.

He had to get out of there. And fast.

TRAVIS HAD ROLLED up the sleeves of his camo shirt and shoved his hands deep into his pockets. He stood in the shadows beneath the log pier and watched the moon rise high into the midnight sky.

The gray-green water of Chesapeake Bay lapped against the Virginia shoreline, throwing up an occasional spray to cool the steamy July night. Tomorrow, he'd get to dress in his civvies. Shorts or jeans, and a beat-up top that would be thin enough and cool enough to deal with the summer heat.

But he wasn't looking forward to it.

The Corps actually expected him to shed his uniform for four to six weeks. Forced R and R to get his body back in shape and his head in the right place. Even two weeks was too long to suit him. It felt like quitting. Like throwing in the towel when he knew there was still some fight left in him.

But what if he didn't have it in him anymore—the

skills, the edge, the drive—the able body and clear-headed mindset to be a captain in Special Ops? If that were the case, he'd have been better off if that explosion *had* killed him.

"Hell." He shook his head and inhaled a deep, steadying breath, focusing his attention on the gentle rocking of the boats anchored beneath the pier. He didn't need to go to that dark place again. Men and women in uniform died every day, not because they wanted to, but because they understood their duty. They fought to survive, to carry out their assignments, driven by the faith put in them by their country and the Corps.

He needed to fight just as hard to carry out his duty.

Because if he couldn't fight his way back to his field service assignment with the Corps, he didn't have a clue about what he would do.

His hometown thought he was some kind of hero. What a joke. He couldn't even help an old buddy get out of a boring night working the fair next week. The Action Man might not be fit for action anymore. How the hell was he supposed to deal with that? It scared him senseless.

But Travis's senses weren't so far gone that he couldn't hear the soft squish of footsteps approaching across the golden sand beach. That he didn't recognize the intruder who'd found his childhood hiding place, even before she spoke.

"Hey, stranger." Tess's familiar voice feathered across his eardrums like a soothing breeze in the night. "Skipping out on your own party?"

"I'm not much of a partier."

The top of her head barely reached his shoulder as she stood barefoot beside him. "Since when?"

Since blowing my body to kingdom come and being sentenced to half a life because I can't function as a man or a Marine should any longer.

He stared sightlessly out into the water. This was as comfortable as he'd been since leaving the hospital at Quantico with his dad and Ethan. This hiding place reminded him of simpler times. Or maybe it was Tess's rock steady presence that had finally taken the edge off his mood.

Travis shrugged. "Since I got tired. Seems I get that way a lot lately."

"It's not surprising. You almost died. You've been through several major surgeries. Months of rehabilitation. Your body's still in the process of healing. You have a right to be tired."

"It's no excuse." He turned to face her. He captured a caramel-colored tendril that blew across her cheek and tucked it behind her ear. "It's no excuse for jumpin' down your throat the way I did this afternoon."

Her smile glinted in the moonlight like a fond memory. "You have many fine qualities, Travis. But patience has never been one of them. Your body needs time. Your spirit, too, from the sound of things."

He nodded and pulled his hand away before sensations of silky hair and warm skin imprinted themselves on his fingertips. "I know Dad's worried about me. Hell, half of Ashton's worried. But I don't know if I can do the vacation thing here. It feels like I'm hiding out, like I'm running from the fight."

"Do you want to hire someone else to do your PT?"

"No. I don't want to admit that I still need four more weeks of physical therapy, period." A bit of the now-familiar frustration licked through his veins again. "My men are in a war zone right now. Hell. They're not even my men anymore. I need to be there. I need to do my job. I'm letting them down."

"Because you nearly lost your leg? Your life? I know you McCormicks live and breathe the military, but do you really have to be a superhero every waking moment?"

"You wouldn't understand, T-bone. There's never been something you wanted so bad for so long that that wanting becomes a part of you."

With a sound that was almost a snicker, she turned away, leaving the shadows of the pier's giant support pylons and heading along the beach, back toward their homes a half-mile away. Her dismissive sigh was a sobering reminder that he really knew how to spoil a mood these days. After grabbing his boots and socks, he followed her down near the water and watched her pick up a small stone. She drew back her right arm, waited for the right moment, and skipped the stone across the waves. Four, five, six hits. Nice.

"Hey, I see you've still got your throwing arm. Did you ever figure out how to hit a curve ball?"

Tess laughed and he felt a little less like the jerk he'd been earlier, a little more like the friend he'd been forever. She scooped up her sandals in her fingers and fell into step beside him. "I don't play much hard-core softball anymore. The hospital has a team, but it's pretty much for fun and not all that competitive. Not like what we played back in school."

"So that's a no?"

"Travis!" She swatted his arm and dashed ahead to pick up a relatively straight piece of driftwood, about three-feet long. She dropped her shoes, turned and lifted the skinny log up onto her shoulder like a baseball bat. "Okay, hotshot," she dared him, "let's see if you still have a curve ball before you start criticizing *my* game."

He laughed. This was what he needed. Something normal. Something familiar. Something that didn't depend on the state of his leg or his questionable ability to play the hero. "You want me to throw you a curve ball?"

The bat danced against her shoulder. "If you think you've still got it in you. Find a rock."

He followed the nod of her head and picked up a palm-size rock. The little lady wanted to play, huh? Travis dropped his boots, spit on the rock and rubbed it smooth between his hands. "I led the baseball team to a state championship my junior year," he reminded her.

"And I led the softball team my senior year." She pointed the bat in his direction, tapped the sand, then put it back on her shoulder. "So far, you're just a bunch of talk, McCormick. Let's see some action."

It didn't take long to get into the spirit of a midnight game of stickball on the deserted beach. With his stronger right leg to brace himself, Travis reared back, went through the dramatic motion of an overhead pitch, then stopped his momentum to toss it underhand. Tess swung and missed, and the rock plopped into the sand behind her.

"What, are you afraid I'm going to actually hit the thing?" She tossed the rock back to him. "Now put it over the plate."

Travis pitched. Tess swung. The smack of rock against wood startled them both into laughter. She jammed the rock into the sand just a few feet in front of her.

Travis snatched up the rock and moved in behind Tess. "You call that a swing?"

"You call that a pitch?" she countered.

"Like this, T-bone." Travis grabbed her by the shoulders and pulled her back against his chest. He tucked his chin against her temple and adjusted the bat over her shoulder. With one hand covering both of hers on the bat, he wrapped his free arm around her waist and turned her so that she was lined up with the imaginary plate. He tossed the rock into the air and swung the bat with her, making solid contact with the rock and driving it deep into Chesapeake Bay. He moved the makeshift bat back up into place and repositioned her, repeating the movement a second time. "You have to swing under it like this so you can drive the ball up instead of down into the ground."

The sharp catch of Tess's breathy sigh reached him over the rustle of waves on the beach. She went still in his arms, except for the curly tendrils of golden brown hair that blew against his cheek.

Travis froze. But he didn't move his hand from the nip of her waist or move his face from the salty fresh dampness that clung to her hair. He didn't want to move. Unless he moved *closer*.

Oh, man. He was in worse shape than he'd thought. This was not normal. If he was in this position with any other woman, he'd be nuzzling her neck right now. He'd be tossing the bat and pulling her down into the sand. He'd slide his hands beneath her shirt and unzip her shorts.

But Travis stood there, holding his breath.

This was Tess! A year off his game couldn't have short-circuited every instinct in him, could it? Hot, needy urges careened through his body, but his brain couldn't make any sense of them. This was so completely not the feeling he usually got hanging out with her. Yet the evidence was right there, nestled against his crotch and stirring things that were better left alone.

Tess Bartlett had a rockin' ass to go along with those tits.

And he wanted them. He wanted her.

Bad.

3

"I'M AFRAID I'm gonna have to cancel our trip out to Longbow Island this week," Hal McCormick's chest-deep sigh revealed the depth of his disappointment.

Travis paused outside the kitchen, leaning on his cane as he eavesdropped on his father's telephone conversation. *Cancel?* His father *loved* fishing.

"That's not it," Hal continued. "From what I hear, the striped bass are biting in the rock piles along the shore. We could catch our limit and have plenty to throw back. . . . Nope, that's not the problem either. There's a line of storms due in mid-week, but everything looks great right now."

Was he hearing things right? Only the threat of severe weather kept his father on dry land these days. As a family, they'd always loved outdoor sports, but since the death of Travis's mother nearly a decade ago, spending time on the water—preferably with a fishing rod in his hand—had become a way of life for his father.

After developing a heart condition, forced retirement from his position as a brigadier general in the USMC's Quartermaster Corps had left widower Hal McCormick with two obsessions. One was his three children, and the other his fishing boat, which seemed to grow larger and newer with each passing year.

Travis tilted his head to spy out the sliding glass doors that faced the presently tranquil waters of Chesapeake Bay. Not a cloud in sight this afternoon. What was his dad up to? Frowning, Travis leaned back toward the archway to the kitchen. He had a bad feeling about this.

"There's nothing wrong with the trawler, either," Hal continued. "I would have loved you and the missus to come visit us but, well, it's Travis. Personally, I'm just grateful he's alive after that explosion. But he's having a hard time with his recovery. It's mental as much as physical if you ask me. You know how hard it is to keep a Marine down when his buddies are in the line of fire. You and I were the same way. A couple decades ago, at any rate." Hal laughed as guilty bile pooled in the pit of Travis's stomach. "Trav won't even consider retirement from Special Ops. If he's not careful, he'll permanently cripple himself doing too much too soon. I need to be here to keep an eye on him."

Well, didn't that make him feel like he was about five years old again? Apparently, Travis wasn't the only McCormick whose life had been altered by the accident.

"Ethan and J.C. helped me get him home, but Ethan has to report back to Quantico to prep for his class on Monday." Travis had thought getting big brother out of the way would mellow out the elevated level of concern around here. Instead, it sounded as if his father was dialing his stress up another notch. "No, Caitlin and her husband couldn't make it," Hal went on. "She's so close to term on her pregnancy, Walter, that I can't ask her to leave Alexandria to take care of her brother. Maybe if she wasn't in her ninth month."

Travis shook his head, cursing silently. He was thirty-three. A grown man. A Marine captain. Not a child. And certainly not a wash-out who needed his daddy or anyone else to babysit him.

He could add guilt to the layers of frustration already weighing him down. Yeah, he had issues. But they were *his* problems to deal with, not his family's. His life might have been put on hold for a year. but they weren't going to suffer the same fate—not on his account.

Travis silently leaned the cane against the wall outside the kitchen. If the Velcro on the brace binding his left leg from thigh to ankle wouldn't have made such a noise, he would have removed it as well to make the illusion complete. As it was, he tugged the frayed edge of his cut-off denim shorts over the top of the brace, fixed a grin on his face to counter the ache in his bones, and strolled into the kitchen to raid the leftovers from last night's party.

"What, am I dying?" Travis teased, unwrapping a tray of cookies on the counter and studying them as though choosing between chocolate chip or ginger snap was the biggest challenge he had to face that day. "You aren't seriously giving up a fishing trip for me, are you?"

Hal covered the receiver with his palm. "You've come home for a reason, son. I'm not about to abandon my duty. Walter understands."

The sweet, spicy cookie he munched on suddenly tasted like sawdust.

Walter. As in General Walter Craddock. One of his father's military cronies. Travis's older brother, Ethan, had once reported to Craddock at the DOD—Department of Defense—at the Pentagon. He was one of the chiefs overseeing personnel assignments. An officer whose recommendation—or lack thereof—could make or break Travis's chances of returning to Special Ops.

Not a man he wanted to appear weak in front of.

Travis swallowed the lump of sawdust and gestured for the phone. "Let me talk to him."

"It's General Craddock."

Travis took heed of both the concern and the warning in his father's blue eyes. "I'll make sure I salute."

"Uh-huh." Reluctantly, Hal turned his attention back to the phone. "Walter, my son would like to have a few words with you. Go easy on him."

Go easy? Hell. Why not just tell the general he was a panty-waist who couldn't cut it in the Corps anymore?

But Travis buried his knee-jerk reaction behind a charming, chilled-out facade. He perched on a barstool at the end of the kitchen counter, taking the weight off his leg so he could concentrate on saying all the right things to reassure both his father and Walter Craddock. "General. Travis McCormick here."

"Captain. I'm sorry to hear about your relapse. Do they have the proper medical facilities there in Ashton? If there's anything Millie or I can do to help, let us know." A touch of something that just might be construed as pity colored the general's voice.

Convincing the doctors, the Corps, his friends and family that he wasn't ready to be put out to pasture was going to be an uphill battle all the way. He might as well draw a line in the dirt right now and start the good fight. Forming a vague plan in his head, Travis watched his father cross the room to check the cookie tray for himself. "The rumors of my demise have been greatly exaggerated, sir. You're not getting rid of me that easily."

"Good to hear. The Corps relies on men like you."

He hoped so. "Actually, General, I need to ask you a favor. From one Marine to another."

"Name it. What can I do for you?"

"You can keep your plans with Dad." Travis let a grin filter into the timbre of his voice. "If you and Mrs. Craddock don't drive down from D.C. tomorrow and give him a chance to try out his new Mainship Trawler, we're going to have a national crisis on our hands. Chesapeake Bay could be overrun with striped bass."

"Travis Harold McCormick…"

Craddock's laugh drowned out his dad's reprimand. "Hal's cramping your style?"

Travis didn't want to make light of his father's concerns; he just didn't want the stress-free retirement his father had earned to be another casualty of Travis's lengthy recovery. "I know he was looking forward to your visit. And trust me, if I can survive four weeks in a Central American jungle with nothing but MRE's and a sidearm, then I can manage a couple of days in a well-stocked beach house with satellite TV and a remote control."

"It's that bad, eh?"

"Save me, sir."

Craddock laughed over a rustle of papers at his desk. "Millie and I *were* looking forward to getting out of the city for a few days."

"There's no need for you and Mrs. Craddock to alter your itinerary on my account."

"I was going to ask your father about bringing along a family friend as well."

"The more the merrier," Travis insisted.

"Unfortunately, that could be a problem. I can't guarantee how merry she'll be."

"She?"

"Eileen Ward. She's my secretary here at the DOD. A civilian."

Was the general playing match-maker to his dad? From the corner of his eye, Travis watched his father studiously debate between the chocolate chips and ginger snaps, then ultimately choose one of each. Was that the old man's idea of conflict and excitement these days?

Though he was a little gray on top, and definitely set in his ways, Hal McCormick was still in pretty decent fighting shape. He had pills he took regularly for his heart, but his outdoorsy hobbies and regimented diet—okay, so he still had a weakness for sweets—kept him trim. According to a few articles Travis had read, a sixty-year-old man in his father's relatively sound health and secure financial position made a pretty good catch. Still, he'd remained steadfastly unattached since being widowed. He didn't date, didn't flirt. He just…fished.

Travis frowned as Hal gazed out the window above the sink and chewed. Was his father content with his early retirement? Was he bored? Lonely? Looking for action? Did Hal McCormick even remember what *action* was?

Eeuw.

Travis cringed, remembering his own body's wildly inappropriate reaction to Tess Bartlett yesterday afternoon and last night on the beach. His skin prickled with an instantaneous, self-conscious awareness as he recalled vivid details from the erotic dreams that had haunted him through the night.

His and Tess's second-floor bedrooms faced each other. Only, instead of replaying their silly childhood hand signals that they'd once used to communicate with each other after lights-out, he'd pictured her trim, athletic body standing buck naked in her window. Definitely all grown up. And the gestures she'd sent across the moonlit night between them had all been provocative invitations. In his dreams, she'd touched herself, pleasured herself, served herself up on a silver platter for him to watch and want. And then they'd been on the beach together. In the water. In his bed. He'd been inside her mouth. Inside her body. He'd tasted her from stem to stern. She'd tasted him. He'd been the Action Man in his prime, and she'd been his match in every sexy, seductive way possible.

In his dreams.

Travis had awakened, tangled in his covers, feeling hot and achy and unsatisfied. And mortally concerned that he'd been fantasizing about his best friend in such a raw, uncensored fashion. Apparently, a year of recuperation had taken its toll on his sanity as well as his body. He'd certainly found that out at the beach last night. The only thing that had stopped him from taking her for a roll in the sand had been her reluctant but necessary suggestion that they should get back to the party.

Friend or no, did his father have fantasies about a woman the way Travis had about Tess? Did Hal ever crave that kind of action?

Did Travis really want to be thinking about *father* and *action* in the same sentence?

"Damn."

"McCormick?"

Focus.

Travis shifted on the barstool, uncomfortably aware that his life was completely out of whack. He hadn't done a very good job of taking care of himself this past year. He didn't intend to jeopardize his future friendship with Tess by listening to his lusty hormones.

But in the here and now, he could pull it together and help his dad. He had a sneaking suspicion that Hal McCormick had put his whole life on hold for the sake of his children—the same way he wanted to put this fishing trip on hold.

Pulling his shoulders back to attention, Travis concentrated on a brand new strategy. Time to redirect the opposition. He raised the volume of his voice so Hal could hear every word. "Tell me more about this Eileen who's coming with you."

"Eileen?" Hal stopped mid-chew and frowned. "Who's Eileen? What happened to Millie?"

Good. His father's attention had just shifted to a new topic. Travis patted the air with a placating hand, silently telling him not to worry, yet secretly glad he was distracted.

General Craddock gave the low-down. "Eileen's been with me for years. Works her butt off. She's not much for socializing, but her ex is getting re-married this weekend, and Millie thinks Eileen needs to get out and meet some people instead of moping at home."

Hmm. Depressed hermit. Obsessed with work. Been with the general for years. Eileen sounded like a real stick in the mud. Maybe he wouldn't have to worry about that bothersome picture of his sixty-year-old father getting some action. "Does she enjoy being on the water?" Travis asked.

Unable to stop his curiosity, Hal brushed the crumbs from his hands over the sink, then crossed close enough to whisper, "This woman's coming here with Walter?"

Travis hushed his voice as well. "It's his secretary, Dad. Millie and Eileen are both coming."

"I have no idea what her hobbies are, besides the plants she always has on her desk. She doesn't talk about her personal life much." Craddock's tone altered with a mix of apology and admiration. "I don't know if you remember my wife, but Millie can be quite formidable once she sets her mind to a thing."

It was Travis's turn to laugh. He'd heard that Millie Craddock had played a small but key role in getting his brother, Ethan, and his wife, J.C., together.

"I remember her." Mrs. Craddock's determination might prove his best ally when it came to easing his guilt. Whether this Eileen proved date-worthy or not, Travis would see to it that his father didn't sacrifice one more thing on his account. "It doesn't sound wise to disappoint the missus, sir. You come on down to Ashton and bring your guest. Dad will appreciate the company." Now for the lie. He raised his voice a notch. "I've got plans myself, anyway. Dad'll be here by himself if you don't come."

Hal rested a warning hand on Travis's shoulder. "What plans?"

Travis winked to reassure his dad, but spoke to the general. He was making this up as he went along. He may have a bum leg, but his bullshit skills were completely intact. "I have a class reunion thing going on, meeting with some high school friends." Why not go all the way? "I promised I'd help them with the Bay Festival this week. I don't know why Dad wants to hang around the house—I'll be gone most of the time, anyway."

Hal's grip tightened. "When did you make these plans? The doctor said you needed rest."

"Rest *and* recreation, Dad. This is the recreation part. Besides, I'll be hangin' with Tess. I can't get any safer than that, can I?" Travis offered a brief explanation to the general. "One of my classmates just happens to be my physical therapist. She'll keep an eye on me."

"You're sure?"

Positive. "What time shall I tell Dad to expect you?"

Though Hal knew his younger son well enough not to be completely swayed by his reassurances, he seemed to reclaim some of his excitement when he got back on the phone to make final arrangements with General Craddock. "I guess we're still on then, Walter. If Trav has Tess to watch over him, he'll be all right. She's a good kid. Who's this Eileen person? Does she know her way around a boat?"

Travis excused himself and headed for the front door, pulling his cell phone from the waistband of his cut-offs. He took a short-cut across the yard as he punched in a familiar number. He had to get ahold of Tess. He needed to shove aside the lust still sparking through his system and ask his old buddy for a favor.

Schedule me a PT time. Get me out of the house and keep me occupied long enough so that Dad will quit hovering and go back to living his own life. Travis needed an alibi so that the story he'd just told his father and the general wouldn't make a complete liar out of him.

He was dragging his sorry leg up the back steps to the Bartlett's patio door before anyone answered. "Hello?"

"T-bone."

"Trav?"

Searching through the sliding glass door, he spotted her in the kitchen and breathed a momentary sigh of relief. But then his pulse hammered into overdrive as he shamelessly watched her through the window. She wasn't naked; she wasn't pleasuring herself the way she had in his dreams. But suddenly he was drop-dead stupid with want for her. He edged closer to the window.

Tess wore a Washington Nationals baseball jersey with Frank Robinson's number on it. Classic choice. But just like last night on the beach, he couldn't concentrate on baseball. Either that jersey was way too long, or her shorts were way too short—because he was looking at nothing but smooth, tanned skin on that long stretch of thighs. Capped off by the swells of her sweet backside when she bent over to pull a tin of muffins from the oven, the only thing he could think of was bending her over the counter and getting a little sugar for himself.

Tess frowned as she straightened and tossed off the oven mitt. She pulled the phone from where she'd wedged it between her ear and shoulder. "Travis? Are you there?"

He saw a glob of batter dotting her cheek when she craned her neck to look through the west windows toward his house. That glob should have reminded him of the food fight they'd had in junior high school and how going to the office together as comrades-in-arms had been one of their first bonding experiences. Instead, he wanted to lick off that batter and find out if the skin beneath tasted just as sweet.

"Travis?"

"Forgive me for anything I've ever done to you." Including lusting after you like a Marine who's just seen his first female in twelve months.

"What are you talking about?"

Travis curled his fingers into his palm and tapped on the glass to get her attention. When she turned, her familiar smile of recognition and welcome warmed him down to his toes like a comfortable hug, and some of that unexpected obsession shouting through his veins quieted. Yeah, T-bone would help him out.

But as she hung up the phone and approached, images of other recent hugs surfaced. The tight knots of those perky breasts smushed against his chest. The streamlined curve of her bottom snugged against his groin. Nerve endings and cell membranes and even bigger body parts leaped to attention at the thought of her stopping on her side of the window and stripping down to make his erotic dreams come true.

Son of a bitch. Travis slapped his phone shut against his temple, ending the call and knocking some sense into his head. Where were these impulses coming from? Why now? Why Tess?

He stepped back onto the patio as she opened the door—without undoing a single button. "What's going on?"

"I want your ass."

Shit. Had that just come out of his mouth?

Tess's green-gold eyes widened. "Excuse me?"

Smooth one, McCormick.

Travis swallowed hard, silently dressed down his libido and articulated his request as though he'd never uttered any indication of his crazy new attraction to her. "I need you to save *my* ass."

CAPTAIN KYLE BLACK knocked on the door frame marking Walter Craddock's office and ushered himself inside as the general hung up the phone.

He carried in the report Craddock hadn't asked for until next week and set it on his desk. Seventeen hundred hours was generally quitting time, but it was never too late in the day to make an impression on his commanding officer. "Taking off for the weekend, sir?"

Craddock nodded as he leaned back in his chair. "Actually, I'm heading out of town with Millie for a few days. Eileen's coming with us, too. I've decided the only way to get that woman to take a vacation is to order her to."

"She's not military, sir."

"Well, I won't hold it against her." Kyle grinned at the general's dry humor. "We'll be back in the office Tuesday morning."

"I'll hold down the fort while you're gone, sir," Kyle reassured him. He'd gotten assigned to the general's office six months earlier. If Kyle's career plan stayed on track, he'd make major and be running his own staff within the year. Moving up the chain of command was as much about making nice with the man who headed up the Corps's promotions committee as it was doing an impeccable job. So he asked, "Where you headed?"

"Ashton, Virginia." The general rose, tucking his khaki shirt into his green gabardine slacks.

Damn, Kyle thought. That's where the traitor lived.

Anticipating the general's every need, Kyle retrieved his gold-trimmed, flat-topped hat from the stand beside the door. "Down on Chesapeake Bay?"

"You're familiar with the place?"

Judging by the general's questioning squint, Kyle must have revealed something in his own expression. Handing over the hat, Kyle held the smile on his face as if the mention of Ashton, Virginia, hadn't just twisted like a hot knife in his back.

"I've been there before." Twice, to be precise. The first time had been with his buddies during their first leave from Officers Training School at Camp LeJeune. He'd learned who his real friends were then. And who his real competition was.

Travis McCormick had walked around as if he were in a spotlight 24/7. The others in their unit had looked to the Action Man, not Kyle, for leadership, even though he'd earned just as many ribbons and points of distinction. Because he'd been flashier, drawn more attention to himself, McCormick had received the first promotion, drawn the coveted assignment to Special Ops—gotten the girl.

But because he was all about precise planning and perseverence, Kyle had returned to Ashton a second time. With a purpose. On a very personal mission.

He'd been shot down in flames. Made a fool of. Because of Travis McCormick. Again. Damn, what he wouldn't give to make that right.

But instead of venting any history, Kyle scratched his fingers across the back of his coal black crew cut and feigned nothing more than a passing knowledge of the place. "It's one of those quaint little towns on the southern coast, right off the Atlantic. They have a big fair and celebration there every summer, don't they? Is that where you're headed?"

Craddock tucked his hat beneath his arm and headed toward the door. "The Summer Bay Festival. Starts Monday. Frankly, I'm hoping to avoid all the hoopla. I'm going down to hang with an old buddy of mine, Hal McCormick. I hear the fish are biting."

"McCormick?" The knife in Kyle's back twisted down to the hilt.

Craddock paused and glanced over his shoulder. "You know the Brigadier?"

The brigadier. Right. Kyle resumed his veneer of indispensable efficiency and shrugged. "By reputation only, sir. I was aide to his son, Ethan, until his transfer to Quantico. Then I came to your office."

"That's right. Lieutenant Colonel McCormick's recommendation is why I selected you for this assignment."

At least one brother had done right by him. "I appreciate that, sir. Did you and General McCormick serve together?"

His superior's craggy face eased into a smile. "For a lot of years. Hal owes me at least one trip on his boat."

Travis McCormick owed Kyle a lot more than that. But Kyle had no intention of letting anything but friendly respect show in his face and posture. "Then I'll say, 'Bon voyage.' You'd better hit the road unless you enjoy the rush hour traffic out of D.C."

The general strode through the doorway. Kyle paced after him, turning toward his desk. But Craddock's curse stopped him before he reached his chair. "Did Eileen leave already?"

"She was taking those files down to the JAG's office on her way out." Kyle reached for the phone on the corner of his desk. "You want me to page her?"

"No, if she just left, I'll run her down." The general hesitated at the door. "If my wife calls, tell her…hell, I was supposed to talk to Eileen before she left. Tell her—"

"—You're heading straight home after you touch base with Mrs. Ward? I'll call the JAG's office to detain her, just in case."

Craddock smiled. Point scored. "You're a good man, Black. You got plans this weekend?"

Kyle nodded. He always had a date.

"Enjoy it."

"Thank you, sir." They traded salutes and the general left. As soon as he finished the call to the JAG office, Kyle was pulling up a duty assignment on his computer.

Kyle scanned the information on the screen, memorizing every detail. Captain Travis McCormick had been assigned a six-week medical leave, following six months in hospital and six months on light duty at Quantico. Six weeks? Medical? Someone was worried. If he knew McCormick, he'd be bustin' his butt to turn that leave into four weeks, or even two.

"You're not Superman anymore, are you?" he taunted the computer monitor in lieu of McCormick's face.

Kyle had plans, all right. But the model he'd been seeing the past two weeks held little interest for him at the moment. He was too busy typing in the necessary info to request a temporary leave himself. Just a few days. The Summer Bay Festival and its draw of military personnel from up and down the East Coast would provide the perfect cover. Once General Craddock returned, Kyle would hit the road for Ashton himself. He could do a few scouting jaunts beforehand, learn McCormick's routine, devise a plan.

To Kyle's way of thinking, this wasn't about striking a man while he was down. It was about locating the enemy's vulnerability and using that weakness to his advantage to ensure victory.

It was about payback.

4

"A LITTLE HELP?" Tess grabbed Travis's unshaven jaw and turned his appreciative gaze away from Robin, the brunette ward clerk who'd retrieved his signed consent form with a wink and an encouraging smile. With the door to the otherwise empty PT room closing on the distraction of Robin's backside, Tess pointed to her own eyes. "Right here, McCormick. Concentrate."

"Come on, T-bone. I haven't had a chance to play for twelve months." He offered up a "poor me" look as he leaned back against the weight machine's padded seat. "Don't begrudge a wounded man the chance to get out and see the sights. The hospital's new PT wing really *does* have nice scenery."

"So does the Grand Canyon. Which I'm tempted to shove you into if you don't start taking this seriously."

"I had a drill sergeant like you once."

Tess ignored the teasing gibe. "Screwing around could get you hurt."

"I think my mother gave me the same advice back in high school."

"Travis," she snapped. He could joke around about this all he wanted, but she'd seen his X-rays. She knew how far he'd come and how far he still had to go. It was a precarious balance of strengthening the right muscles while protecting weaker ligaments and knitted bones. Healing was dead serious business, and if he truly wanted to return to hazardous duty as a Marine in just a couple of weeks, then it was her responsibility to keep him from doing any more damage to himself on the homefront. "If we don't do this right, there's no sense doing it at all."

"Yes, sir." He snapped her a salute. "Doing it right, sir."

Tess rolled her eyes. "Whatever."

Securing Travis's feet beneath the T-bar, she tested the resistance on the machine to make sure the pressure rested on his thighs and calves instead of his rebuilt knee and ankle. She braced her hand against the muscles beneath his nylon workout pants.

"I'm still in pretty good shape, right?" Though couched as a taunt, Tess knew him well enough to hear the underlying need for validation in his tone.

She adjusted the machine, then repositioned his leg and guided him to try the weight. "Robin seemed to think so."

"Yeah, but she never saw the *before* picture."

"Trust me. I knew you before the accident, and you are still…"

Hot got stuck in her throat when she lifted her face and met his gaze. She'd intended to give him a reassuring smile, but snapping shut her mouth, which had fallen open at the look on his face, was all she could manage at the moment. There was nothing teasing in the deep blue eyes that focused on her now. The veil of laughter had disappeared, revealing a raw need in the depths of those cobalt irises. They were as complex and unfamiliar as they'd been yesterday afternoon, ogling her with a hungry intensity that made her hair sweat.

If she'd been another woman, Tess might have interpreted the rare glimpses of serious emotion as some sort of intimate, passionate, man-woman connection.

But she was Tess Bartlett. Trusty sidekick. Go-to woman when a friend needed a favor.

He was Travis McCormick. The Action Man. A nickname that had as much to do with his reputation with the ladies as it did his heroics for his country.

All he'd ever wanted from her was a bud to listen to him, to back him up, to have fun with—someone to give him a boost behind the scenes so he could still face the world with a charming smile whenever things fell apart.

That's what the searching glance, the glimpse of vulnerability, was all about. It was a silent plea to the friendly ally she'd always been. He needed someone to bolster his ego as he learned to cope with limitations he'd never had to face before.

Tess swallowed hard and looked away to focus her attention on the movement of his leg. She couldn't keep it casual and supportive when she wanted that look to mean something else.

"You're lookin' pretty fine," she assured him, saying what he needed to hear. It wasn't a lie. Despite the ribs of scar tissue she felt through his pant leg, the shape and dimension of the muscles underneath were the same grade-A prime that had always set countless female hormones, including her own, into overdrive. Sure, his obvious pain—past and present—triggered her compassion. But there was no reason to feel sorry for this man.

His fingers brushed across the back of her knuckles. Nerves jumped. Muscles tightened. Her mouth went dry. "You're sure 'bout that? You had to think about it."

Did she imagine that low-pitched husk in his voice? Or had he always had that sexy rumble?

"I'm positive," she croaked, then snatched her hand away and cleared her throat. "You are all that, and a bag of chips. And not that cheap store-brand stuff, either. You're name brand, all the way."

If her playful comeback sounded forced, Travis didn't seem to notice. Of course, Tess didn't really bother to check. She smoothed her damp palms on her khaki shorts and turned away to fiddle with the weights before the static charges zipping from his body to her brain completely short-circuited her ability to perform her professional duty. At least one of them needed to keep track of why they were here. Resolving to ignore both the intensity of those eyes and the seduction of that voice, she patted the top of his thigh. "Let's try it again, nice and slow this time so I can gauge your range of motion."

"Yes, sir." Now *that* was the smart-ass tone she'd come to expect from him. Still, touching him made it hard to concentrate. His thigh tightened like a rock beneath her palm as he extended his legs. "I noticed Robin wasn't wearing a wedding ring. Is that a job thing? So she doesn't catch a finger in one of these machines or scratch a patient?"

"Subtle, McCormick."

Like the ebb and flow of the tide, the muscle thinned as he relaxed his thigh back into place. He repeated the motion. Flexed. Hard. Filling her hand. Relaxed. She caught her breath, waiting in subconscious anticipation for the hard muscle to swell into her palm again. "So, is she unattached?"

"Travis." She swatted the provocative flesh and stepped back to prop her hands at her hips. She didn't need this kind of interrogation to taunt her ego while he tempted her libido. "You're the one who insisted we start physical therapy this weekend. You know, as impossible as it is for you to believe, I *do* have a life. I don't normally give up my Saturday afternoons. Even for a friend." She flipped her ponytail from inside the collar of her uniform polo shirt, begrudgingly admitting to herself that she didn't really have that much of a life to back up her argument. Pathetic. "Robin's not married. And she isn't seeing anyone exclusively that I know of."

"Interesting."

Tess concentrated on her breathing, in and out, so she wouldn't stand there holding her breath, waiting for Travis to ask her to set him up on a date with Robin. The clerk had certainly sent out signals that she would be interested in getting better acquainted with the captain.

Travis unhooked his feet from the T-bar and dropped them to the floor so he could turn and fiddle with the machinery behind him. "I can handle more weight, you know."

Tess frowned at the back of his head. She was as perplexed by his abrupt change in subject as she was relieved. The Action Man she knew would never have passed on such an easy opportunity to hook up with an attractive woman.

But then, the flirtatious hero she once knew had been an unpredictable man since coming home from Quantico. This man got angry. This man hesitated. There was a chink in the confidence that had once exuded from every pore. A chink that revealed an edge to Travis she'd never seen before. When she'd sent him off to college, to basic training, to officer candidate school, to assignments across the country and across the world, he'd always been cocky but in control—a man who knew who he was, knew what he wanted, knew what he was capable of. He was a man who delivered each and every time—and took pride in that fact.

Had his brush with death really changed him? Or was this version of Travis merely the golden boy finally growing up and learning that he was human like everybody else?

If the former golden boy had been lust-worthy, this moodier, edgier Travis touched something deeper inside her. The old Travis had needed nothing. No one. This one needed…something.

And whether it was a friendly hug, a roll in the hay or a kick in the pants, she wanted to be the one to give it to him.

She wanted to be what he needed.

Burying her own pointless urges, Tess pulled his hand from the weights at the back of the machine. "We're not pushing anything until I'm certain you won't cause more damage to that knee."

Travis stood, butting her shoulder as he moved past her. "The main reason I'm here is to keep Dad happy. He thinks I need a nursemaid."

"So you're here for your dad, not yourself?"

"There's nothing you can do for me that I can't do for myself."

"I can monitor your progress." She shook her head at the mark where he'd set the leg press. He'd locked in a weight that would challenge even a completely healthy man. "Keep you from hurting yourself."

"I know what I did wrong," he insisted. "I'll be more careful this time." He circled the weight-training equipment, eyeing each machine as if it were an enemy he'd defeated in battle who'd come back to haunt him. What was going on?

"Gee, and here I thought my license, two college degrees and a few years experience meant *I* was the expert." She hoped sarcasm would snap him out of this weird funk. "Sounds like I've been working too hard."

He raised his hands in apologetic surrender. "I didn't mean it like that. I'm sure you're good at what you do. It's just…hospitals and therapy centers get pretty boring after a while. I need to be back at Quantico in two weeks when my unit returns stateside. Not even you can work a miracle in that time. I'm either ready now, or I'm out."

Though she questioned his self-diagnosis, Tess smiled to show she'd taken no real offense. "You don't want therapy, despite your doctor's recommendation. So why are we here?"

As he stood facing her, she saw that the worn cotton of his gray USMC T-shirt clung just as snugly to the swells and planes of his chest and torso as it had to his broad shoulders and trim back. But the instant she let her admiration slide down to his legs, he turned away and resumed his pacing.

"I'm here so that my family will get on with their lives. Ethan took time off from work to haul me around, Caitlin and Sean rescheduled an appointment with her ob-gyn because she was worried I wouldn't fix three meals a day for myself." He jabbed at a punching bag, trailed his fingers up and down the railing on a set of practice stairs and wound up in front of one of the therapeutic massage tables. "They've all put their own lives on hold so that they can look after me. It's damn embarrassing to still feel like an invalid a year after that bomb…"

The tension radiating off his body demanded that she go to him. "They love you. Families worry. That's what they do."

"Mine worries too much. They…" Tess reached for his shoulders and dug her fingers into the cords of stress there. "Hell." He jerked beneath her touch, then his posture deflated and he leaned forward, bracing his arms on top of the table. "Okay. We could do this for two weeks. God, you're good."

"Told you so." She kneaded her thumbs into the knots of tension lining his shoulder blades. "Lie down. If you're this tight all over, you're bound to pull something."

"I've been a bear. You don't have to."

"I'm in charge of this therapy session. Lie down," she ordered.

Tess never broke contact as he settled, belly-down, on the table. As she worked along his spine, the soft cotton of his T-shirt provided little barrier between her hands and the hard skin that warmed beneath her touch. He was as beautiful to touch as he was to look at, and Tess found herself closing her eyes and savoring the discovery of heat and shape and textures.

"Maybe it's counseling you need instead of physical therapy," she suggested, massaging each muscle until she felt the tension break and relax. "I could recommend someone from the hospital staff."

When her fingers found the hem of his T-shirt, she bunched it up and slid her palms across smooth, hot skin. He shivered, and she didn't think it was entirely due to the room's air conditioning.

"Oh, yeah, T-bone," he murmured, pointedly ignoring her suggestion. "Just like that. Gives a man ideas."

Touching him like this was giving *her* ideas, and none of them were of the Girl Friday, kid sister, trusty sidekick kind. Nah, she was thinking more along the lines of summer fling.

She stroked the bare skin along his flanks, letting the sensitive pads of her fingers find each goose bump and soothe it into submission. She traced the hard line of his spine, and pushed her fingers into the flare of muscle rising toward his buttocks.

Oh, yeah was right.

But Travis still wanted to talk.

"Trust me, I've seen plenty of shrinks, too." His voice slurred against the frame that cushioned his face. "All I need is a chance to get back to the job I do best and prove to everyone I've still got what it takes."

"To be a Marine?"

"Yeah," he moaned in a mix of pain and pleasure. "That's the spot." Tess slipped her tiring fingers beneath the elastic barrier of his pants and briefs to knead the small of his back. "When I was finally deemed fit, they reassigned me to light duty. I trained to be a Marine, not a paper-pusher. Every job's important—don't get me wrong—it takes every last man and woman for the Corps to run like the well-oiled machine it is. But I was bred for the front line. Special Ops. That's where I was meant to be."

"Aren't there other jobs in the Corps that could be just as exciting and rewarding?"

"No."

Tension crept back beneath her fingertips at the stark answer.

Tess opened her eyes. "And you resent your family worrying about you?"

"I resent my father putting his life on hold because he thinks I'm going to crash and burn without his constant supervision. I don't think he's ever gotten over not being at the hospital when Mom died. I think he's afraid he's going to lose me, too, if he lets me out of his sight."

"So you recruited me to get you out of the house?"

"It was the first thing I could think of. He trusts you." He shifted on the table, unwittingly thrusting her fingers farther beneath the band of his briefs. "I knew you'd come through for me."

Her hands burned as she battled the urge to squeeze the devilishly firm cheeks right there beneath her palms. "You want me to be your accomplice, not your therapist."

Tess pulled her wandering hands back to neutral territory by tucking them beneath her arms.

"I need you to be my friend." Travis rolled onto his side to face her, apparently unaffected by their skin-to-skin contact the way she was. "If you'll provide an excuse for me, Dad, Ethan and Caitlin will go on with their normal lives. They trust you to look out for me. If they think I'm in your care, that we're working together..." He wrapped his fingers around her forearm and pulled himself up. "You're the only one I can count on. I'll make it up to you. I promise."

"How? You're asking me to lie to a man who's been like a second father to me. Why can't we just do the therapy for two weeks?"

"Because it doesn't work!" Travis pounded the table and Tess jumped at the power of his frustration. Instantly, his eyes darkened with shadows of regret. Softening his tone, he held up his hands and apologized. "Sorry. Usually, I can keep it in check."

"You don't have to cover up what you think or feel with me. We're buds." She curled one hand into a fist and held it out in a familiar gesture between friends.

Travis stared at her offering as if he didn't remember— or no longer believed—what it meant. His weary sigh hinted at the latter. But his wry smile matched hers as he fisted his own hand and tapped it against hers. "Buds."

Tess pulled away and hooked her thumbs into the pockets of her shorts. "You want me to lie to Hal and tell him that you and I are working hard at this recovery that you don't really want to work on at all."

"I want to recover, make no mistake." He rubbed his hand along his injured thigh. "But I reported to physical therapy for six months and worked out on my own time, too. And what happened? The day before they're going to test me and rate me fit for S.O. duty, I rip my knee up again. It's weak. I'm weak."

Her eyes couldn't help but roam. In what earthly way could a man built like a battle-ready Achilles possibly be considered weak? Not the point. Tess blinked and drew her gaze back to his. "So, you're thinking if six months with the United States Marine

Corps couldn't fix you up, then six weeks with me is obviously a waste of your time."

"Time spent with you is never a waste," he assured her. Once she smiled, so did he. "But this is my battle—my head game, my body. I don't want Dad and my family, or you," he winked, "to become casualties of my mission."

"To get back to Special Ops."

Travis nodded.

Fine. He didn't want her help in her one area of expertise. But she was determined to help him. After all, that was what friends did. Maybe she could sneak in some physio-training—recruit him to help rearrange the furniture in her old bedroom, or lure him into the water to clean and put some touch-up paint on one of Hal's boats. "So tell me what the deal is. What do I get out of this arrangment?"

"I can recruit some buddies from the base to cover your shift at the festival so you can have time off. Or I'll teach you how to hit that curve ball. Anything you want. Just keep me busy and out of my family's hair." He pressed his hands together in supplication. "Please."

"Anything?" Would he make love to her? Now that would give him the cardio workout he needed to maintain peak physical stamina. Would he look at her with lusty intent the way he did every other woman on the planet? Could he teach her whatever secret spark she lacked that made men ask her for a favor instead of sexual favors?

"Anything."

Damn, those blue eyes were serious.

Her skin erupted in a sea of goose bumps at the suggestive promise in his voice. Would he? Did she have the guts to ask for what she really wanted? Was it foolish to jeopardize their relationship? Or was asking a friend to train her in the ways of seduction, instead of waiting for Mr. Right to come along and do it, the smartest move she could make?

"Cold?" He'd spotted the goose bumps on her arms, and immediately, familiarly, his hands were there, rubbing gently up and down her arms.

"Feeling a little warm, actually."

She stopped the massage by lacing her fingers through his. Their hands were both strong and muscular, but the contrasts between them were obvious. Size. Length. The sprinkling of golden hair at his wrist, the faint dusting of fine tawny hair on her own. His scarred knuckles and blunt nails. Her paler skin.

There'd be similar contrasts elsewhere on their bodies. If they kissed. If they got close. If they meshed together.

Tess's pulse raced at the possibilities.

"What are you up to, T-bone?" he whispered, studying the link of their hands as well.

Her lips moved before her brain and almost two decades of friendship could stop her. "How about we swap training exercises? I'll schedule times for this *therapy* you're not having, and you could teach me—"

Her cell phone rang from her bag across the room, interrupting her thoughts, stifling her courage to ask Travis for an affair.

"Saved by the bell." His words were meant to be a joke, but the tension in the room didn't dissipate.

Tess broke away. She pulled the phone from her back-pack, checked the number and groaned before answering. "Hey, Morty."

"Tess," Morty Camden greeted in his businesslike tone. "How's your weekend going?"

"Fine. What do you need?"

"What do I need?" Morty hesitated. "Is everything okay?"

Tess pressed a hand to her temple and shoved a stray tendril behind her ear. "Sorry to snap. I just know that if you're calling this close to the start of the festival that there's a problem of some kind."

"Well, it's not a problem, exactly. I mean, it's not about the festival. I need to ask you a favor."

Who didn't?

Why else would Morty be calling—why else would any man be calling—if not to ask *her* to solve *his* problem? Still, Tess strove to hold a charitable thought. "What's the favor?"

"I'm free the second night of the fair. And I was wondering…"

Tess's hand stilled on her ponytail. Was he asking her out? Even though it was sweet, reliable Morty, and not hot, unattainable Travis, who had singled her out, she still felt a rare flutter of anticipation. A genuine date *would* take her mind off this crazy obsession with Travis. "Wondering what?"

"Does your sister, Amy, have any plans?"

The momentary bubble of hope burst. "Are you kidding? You want me to ask Amy out for you?"

"Ouch." Travis's sympathetic comment behind her made her embarrassment complete.

"Would you?" Morty hurried to explain his concern. "I know she's recently divorced, and maybe she's not ready to date anyone. But I'd keep it casual. And we had such a delightful conversation at Travis's party Thursday night, I thought maybe she'd enjoyed my company as much as I enjoyed hers. But if you could provide that little buffer…"

Tess made a valiant effort to set aside her own feelings and think of Amy's current disregard for the male species. Morty was shy, but sincere. It wasn't as though he was a player, like Amy's ex. Amy had talked about going to the carnival and checking out the shops, anyway—and with Tess working an extra night, she wouldn't be able to spend that time with her sister. She couldn't begrudge Amy a chance to go out just because *her* life was booked.

"Call her this evening, Morty." Tess gave her blessing and urged him to show a little backbone at the same time. "You do the asking. But I'll have put in a good word for you by then."

"Thanks, Tess." The accountant sounded almost giddy with relief. "I owe you one."

Get in line.

They traded goodbyes and she disconnected the call.

"Why didn't you tell him to stick it?" She turned around to see Travis sitting on the edge of the massage table, his legs veed out in a casual position that belied the pinpoint stare of his alert, ever-observant eyes.

Shrugging off his protective concern, Tess crossed back to the table. "It's just Morty. He didn't mean it to come off like an insult."

"That's bull. A man doesn't call a woman to ask somebody else out for him."

"You did it."

"Back in high school and college days," he argued.

"I didn't ask you to set me up with Robin just now. Morty's a grown man."

Tess swept a lock of hair off her face and planted her fists on her hips. Mr. Man-of-the-World just didn't get where she was coming from. "Trav, I've been the plain-old tomboy next door for so many years that it's impossible for the men in this town to see me in any other way. I've tried to shake the stereotype, but I can't. They ask me to be their friend or to do them a favor. But they don't ask me out."

Travis reached for her. He startled a noisy gasp from her as his big hands spanned her waist and pulled her between his legs. "Then the men of Ashton are idiots."

Her hands had nowhere to brace themselves except against his chest. She curled her fingers into a fistful of cotton and shook him to make her point. "*You* don't see me any other way, either."

He brushed that pesky lock of hair off her cheek and tucked it behind her ear. "Don't be so sure, T-bone."

"Right." She angled her head in disbelief. "You'd ask me out on a date that didn't involve playing baseball and *did* involve making out."

"You want me to?"

Dammit, his voice had changed again. It had dropped to the husky whisper that fanned her pulse into liquid fire and mocked her resolve to keep things light and friendly between them. "I'm serious. Like, I bet right now you couldn't kiss me without breaking into fits of laughter. You'd think you were kissing your sister or the shortstop, and that would be just too weird."

That's what she needed—a good belly laugh to make the need coiling inside her go away.

But the hands at her waist and nape tightened imperceptibly, drawing her closer. He angled his face toward hers. "Are you daring me to kiss you?"

"I'm proving a point." His eyes were close enough for her to see the kaleidoscope of sapphire, cobalt and midnight ringing the black, dilated pupils. She could feel the heat of the afternoon workout through his clothes, smell the hint of musk and soap on his skin. Desire clogged her throat, turning her argument into a breathless plea. "Unless I work a miracle, or leave town and abandon Mom, I'm destined to take Nixa Newhaven's place as the resident spinster of Ashton, Virginia."

"Then let's work a miracle." He studied her lips as if they were one of her famous blueberry muffins and he were a starving man. A deep, pensive breath made his chest rise beneath her hands. "Maybe we just hit on how I can pay you back for helping me with Dad."

"You're going to kiss me?"

"I'm going to show you how to set this town on its ear, make them see you in a whole new light. And we're going to have fun doing it."

"Impossible."

"Well, first you've got to get over that idea." He stroked the shell of her ear, eliciting a shiver that almost made her forget what they were debating. "You have to think of yourself as an irresistible woman."

Tess laughed at the ludicrous suggestion. The whole idea of being *irresistible* made her nervous, too.

"Don't just think it," he ordered in that seductive

pitch, tracing her ear again. "Believe it. Men will see you in a different light."

"Ashton's had thirty-three years to see me in all kinds of lighting, and—" Her throat tightened up on a startled gasp.

He'd dragged his hand along her ribcage, skimming the side of her breast, and now he lingered since he'd discovered she couldn't form words when he touched her there.

"You are irresistible," he repeated, instructing her, praising her—she couldn't tell which.

"I'm not—" He flicked his thumb over the tight bead of her nipple and she choked on her protest. "Trav—" His name rushed out on an embarrassingly breathless sigh.

He brushed soothing fingertips against her neck, pulling her closer even as he continued to play with her breast. Palming her. Squeezing. Flicking. Rolling. She panted at the electric jolts zinging from each caress straight to the thick, heavy heat between her thighs.

"Still dare me to kiss you?"

No. It might prove an embarrassing repeat of that disastrous night in college. But his warm hand felt so… good. His attentions made her feel so…feminine.

She should stop him. "I never actually said—"

His firm lips covered her half-hearted protest and he thrust his tongue inside, sliding it against hers.

Tess held her breath, stunned by the rasp of his tongue, the grip of his hands, the sweep of his lips against hers.

Travis was really kissing…her.

And he was stone cold sober enough to know what he was doing.

She'd been primed for this moment for far too long to find the will within her to resist. She softened her mouth. He groaned with some kind of release and laid claim, and she answered with every rudimentary instinct she possessed.

Digging her fingers into cotton and skin and the man beneath, Tess pulled herself onto her toes and into his body. She slid one arm behind his neck and skimmed the short prickle of his hair with her sensitized palm. Her breasts ached to feel a firmer touch and she rubbed them against his chest, eliciting a groan that echoed her own.

His tongue stroked hers, and she nipped at it to catch it when he retreated to taste the rim of her lips. He laughed in his throat and swept his hands down to cup her bottom and lift her onto his thick thighs and that hot, intimate place in between. "Definitely irresistible."

Tess moaned with years of want that a few short seconds in Travis's embrace couldn't begin to assuage. "What if someone comes in and sees us?" she breathed against his ear.

"It'll jazz up your reputation."

"But…" Any idea of proving points or proper decorum or even preserving friendship was forgotten as he tumbled backward onto the table, dragging her with him so that she spilled on top of him. "Trav!"

But he didn't stop. She didn't retreat. And no one was laughing.

As her pliant body molded to his harder places, he reclaimed her mouth and drove his tongue deep inside. Whatever rationale she'd intended to stand by was dashed away in the full-body press of their kiss.

5

BASE TO McCormick. McCormick, come in! Retreat! Retreat!

Even disguised in his commanding officer's voice, the warning signals firing off inside Travis's head couldn't get through the static of full-blown desire that was short-circuiting every commonsense impulse in his body.

Tess's predictions were wrong. He wasn't laughing. He wasn't thinking of baseball. And he sure as hell wasn't thinking of his sister.

This girl was a natural. Every move he made, she answered back with her lips and a chorus of hot, sexy moans that hummed in her throat. He'd wanted her closer and she'd obliged. No, she'd taken charge with eager abandon. Crawling on top of him, straddling his hips, rubbing those knotted firebrands against his chest and sinking her white hot promise of satisfaction against his throbbing groin.

He tangled his fingers in the caramel silk of her hair and freed it from its twisty thing in the back. The wavy strands fanned around their faces like a privacy curtain, daring him to do what he would to her lush, responsive mouth.

"You're..." she nipped, he thrust, "a great..." he traced her lips with his tongue, she softened beneath his probing touch, "kisser," He finally finished. She angled her mouth and demanded full-on contact, he accepted the challenge. Endless moments passed before they came up for air. "Been practicing?"

"Not much chance of that around here." She pushed her tongue inside, erasing Travis's questioning frown. He wanted to sort out the cryptic comment, but he was too busy losing himself in what had to be one of the best kisses of his life. He'd rank it number one if he only counted the women he remembered.

There'd been one back in college. A fantasy kiss. A mystery woman. He'd never been that drunk before—had wisely never been that drunk since. But whether that make-out session had been the perfect solace for his breakup with Stacy, or just a feverish wet dream, he'd probably never know.

"Travis?" Tess was squiggling again, rubbing choice parts against bits of his anatomy that leaped in eager response.

"I'm with ya." Reality topped fantasies and shadowy memories every time. He tightened his arms around Tess and reclaimed her kiss.

"Mmm," she moaned with a ragged impatience that matched his own. He dragged his lips to her throat to lap at the sound and taste the drumming beat of her pulse beneath his tongue. "Trav—" she gasped, arching her back and inviting his lips into the unbuttoned gap of her shirt.

Retreat! Retreat!

But Travis was ignoring the order in lieu of discovering the exact spot where the taut skin across her collarbone and sternum gave way to the softer swell of a breast. His pulse pounded in his ears and his nose filled with the arousing scents of citrus and sunshine that clung to her hair and clothes. His mind was lost in the moment—lost in the reawakening sense of manhood, potency, virility, success. He was lost in the woman.

She'd dared him to kiss her.

Seemed like a sweet deal. In exchange for putting his father's fears to rest, he could erase a few doubts about that future spinsterhood she questioned. Give her a shot of confidence. Offer a little expert training to make Ashton sit up and notice the new Tess Bartlett he had become aware of. As a bonus, he could explore, fulfill, then finally cast aside this crazy need that had tormented his waking moments as well as his dreams.

Except…nothing in him seemed to be easing, abating. The more contact he had, the more he wanted. He skimmed his hands along the backs of her smooth, sinewy thighs. Up beneath her shorts. Inside her panties where he kneaded and squeezed a handful of that tight, gorgeous ass.

He tugged her across his chest until one sweet, ripe breast dangled above his mouth. Lifting his head, he captured her nipple through shirt and bra, and suckled until she squirmed and moaned and batted helpless fists against his shoulders.

"Uh-uh, sweetheart," he wanted to coach her. "Don't fight it. Just enjoy."

"Travis—" she gasped. Her fists beat a little harder, but her thighs convulsed around his hips in an unspoken signal of pleasure.

"Touch me." He suckled harder and a tremor racked through her body. "We need…" The cotton knit was wet enough that he could feel the seam of her bra, the puckering of her areola, the needy, greedy thrust of her nipple dancing inside his mouth. "…to touch." He worked his hands between them, unhooking the button of her shorts.

Her fingers slid beneath his shirt, finding and singeing his sensitized skin with her hot, seeking hands. "Like this?"

"Oh, yeah." Travis grabbed at the hem of her pink top. Her back was smooth and supple beneath his hand. He shoved the shirt up and reached for her bra clasp. He wanted a naked, straining tit in his mouth. Now. He fumbled with the hooks. "Damn." He was out of practice. This was going to be a two-handed job.

"We should slow down." She palmed a pectoral. How could he possibly slow down? "Do you think we—?"

"Yes." She brushed her lips against his and he caught them, silenced them. One hook popped. "It's just a kiss." He nipped at her. "Just…" The sensuous curve of her bottom lip fit perfectly between his. "Kiss…"

Pop. The last hook gave way.

He was done talking.

He bucked beneath her, bouncing her up, then sliding his hands inside her shirt and bra, catching her bounty in his palms. She groaned. "This is too much."

It wasn't enough.

He squeezed the dusky tan nipples between his thumbs and forfingers and guided one of them to his eager tongue.

When his teeth got a little nip of the action, her sexy moans erupted into an erotic yelp. He might have laughed when she clapped a self-conscious hand over her mouth, if he wasn't so far gone himself. He rolled, letting her slide onto the table beside him. This was the kind of physical therapy he could get into. This incendiary connection had only one place to go, and he intended to take it all the way. He snatched at her zipper. He'd suffered through hell this past year and had no doubt the solace he'd find burying himself inside Tess would go a long way toward his recovery.

Where the hell had he been for almost twenty years? Not to notice Tess this way? Not to want her like this? This must be summer magic messin' with his head. A moment stolen out of time. It was as if all the surgical teams who'd stitched him back together had altered him somehow. He hadn't been with a woman since the accident. The setting was wrong or the timing was off or he just hadn't been in a friendly mood. But with Tess, in the middle of the afternoon in a public hospital's therapy room…hell, he couldn't get inside her fast enough.

When he reached for his own zipper, he cursed, realizing he wore those damn pants where he had to pull everything down in order to take care of business. Warning her of his intention with another kiss, he twisted himself and lifted her, trying to ease her onto her back so he had room to maneuver. The table stayed rock solid, but his stiff leg protested the sudden acrobatics. A lightning bolt of pain shot through his knee and fired every nerve from his thigh to his hip, effectively stunning all interested parties in between. "Son of a bitch."

Every muscle in him clenched and Travis gritted his teeth, breathing through the aftershocks of pain and frustration. The game had just been called on account of his frickin' body letting him down one more time. Bye-bye, sex. Bye-bye, solace. Bye-bye, Tess.

Hello, reality.

"Trav?" Tess froze, her arms clutched tightly to her exposed breasts. Her voice sounded ragged and distant though she was only inches away. "Did I hurt you?"

"Did you…?" Travis collapsed onto his back beside her and let the colorful commentary rip again. "No. *You* didn't do a damn thing."

They lay side by side on the narrow table, facing the ceiling's fluorescent lights. He still had one arm trapped beneath her shoulders, one hand still splayed with possessive intent atop the dimple of her belly button. The diaphragm muscle beneath his palm rose and fell, indicating the same desperate need for oxygen and sanity that he felt.

She whispered into the charged atmosphere still heating the air around their bodies. "This was a mistake."

No shit. But not because she'd done anything wrong. "I'm the one who screwed up. I let that get way out of hand. I was just supposed to kiss you, not—"

"It takes two to get out of hand." He felt her skin cooling to match the bite in her voice. "Don't move," she ordered. "I'm getting up. If you've reinjured something, I don't want to aggravate it."

"Dammit, T-bone, it's not your fault."

But she was already sitting up on the edge of the table, her back turned as she contorted herself to refasten her bra. Fine. He understood the message: *This is awkward as hell. Promise me we'll never do anything this nutso, out of control again.* He dropped his legs over the edge of the table on the opposite side and sat up.

"Travis! You weren't supposed to move until I check you out."

"I'm fine." Well, mostly. He tugged his T-shirt down and stretched it out to mask the tent in his pants. The Ashton Hospital and its sexiest physical therapist couldn't do anything about *that* problem. "I twisted wrong. It was just a twinge. Now it's gone."

"You're sure?"

"Tess."

She stilled, feeling sufficiently dressed, he supposed, to finally relax. "That was weird, right?"

He tried to think of other women—other men, even—who knew as many secrets and personal baggage about him as Tess did. Besides his sister, there wasn't anyone who came close. He'd been with several women over the years, and had always taken precautions—both the physical and the emotional kind. He knew how to separate fun from intimacy, how to make the act good for both parties without strings being attached. He'd learned the hard way early on that letting his heart get involved in a relationship made him an easy target for heartache. A lover could take his secrets and dreams and walk away. But Tess was loyal to the bone. She was someone who would always be there, someone he could always trust.

He'd never gotten the two categories of women mixed up before.

Travis needed to back way up and think about what he was doing here. "Yeah," he finally dredged up a response. "Weird."

"But I was okay?"

Okay didn't quite describe the fireworks going off

and trains colliding and his dick being as hard as it had been in a year.

"Yeah." The answer didn't feel right. Having this whole conversation didn't feel right. He glanced over his shoulder at the sexy muss of Tess's hair and the shade of embarrassment dotting her cheeks. Through her cotton shirt, he glimpsed the shape of one pebbled nipple, pointing north above the tight hug of her crossed arms. In the south, his penis danced in helpless response. *Okay* was far too tame a word to explain what she had done to his body.

With one finger, he reached out in a peace-making gesture to brush her hair off her neck and drape it behind her shoulder. "I don't get what the men of this town are waiting for if no one's asking you out. You were more than okay. You were hot. You just have to make them see that."

"And you're willing to help?"

"Why not? Fair trade, right? My reputation for yours?"

Her forced laugh grated on his ears. But he caught the hint of a genuine smile when she turned to face him. She pointed to her pink, swollen lips and drew a circle in the air. "You've got a little…"

Travis wiped the back of his hand over his own bruised mouth and came away with streaks of tawny rose lipstick. He grinned. "Nice shade."

He pointed to the unzipped fly of her shorts to return the favor. "And you . . ."

"Oh." Tess glanced down and immediately jumped off the table. Amazing how quickly she could tuck and zip and smooth away the evidence of being so thoroughly groped. "That'd look real professional, wouldn't it?"

He laughed at her sarcasm and ignored the twinge of

discontent nagging at him. Probably guilt. The easy repartee was coming back; he'd better not do anything to spoil it. He eased himself more slowly to his feet. "Not that I was complaining about your bedside manner, but you'd be reprimanded if you showed up for formation looking that sloppy."

"I told you to wait." Tess dashed around the table. Her hands were firm and cool on his shoulder and forearm as she urged him to sit. "I need to check your injury."

Travis shook off the impersonal touch.

"And I told you I was fine." Minding every precise placement of his foot so he wouldn't limp, he headed for the bench where his towel, keys and wallet lay. "It's nothing but a charley-horse. I'll walk it off."

"You're a lousy liar. No wonder you need my help fooling your dad."

He grabbed the towel and flicked it her direction then draped it over his arm in front of him. "For your information, I'm a damn good liar. You're just better at reading me than most people."

She threw her hands up in the air. "There's no way I can convince you to come back here for real physical therapy?"

He glared. "Read this."

"Okay, so you're not an invalid. My mistake." She laughed at his effort to look tough, and things almost felt normal again. Almost.

He still had one pesky problem to take care of. But he managed to grab his keys and wallet and stroll toward the exit without giving himself away. "I'm gonna run home and take a shower." He'd have to finish what they'd started by hand. "We probably should talk a little strategy, get our story straight for Dad and negotiate other ways I can repay the favor." He paused at the exit and turned. "You know, I don't think you need as much practice as you think in the...sexy...department."

"You couldn't tell how out of practice I was? Pickin's are mighty slim here in Ashton."

"They won't be when the fleet comes in next week."

A laugh snorted through her nose. "You want me to trust this sexual makeover to some stranger I meet at the carnival or in a bar?"

No. Definitely not. Travis squeezed his eyes shut and fought to block out the disturbing image of a dozen uniformed men trying to get at what Tess had just offered him on that table. No frickin' way. A woman looking to brush up her sexual image was a prime target for a man to take advantage of. At the very least, he owed her some sort of watch-dog protection. Maybe he could screen the candidates for her. He could at least give her some tips on self-defense if something should get out of hand. "You got plans tonight?"

When he opened his eyes, she was on her hands and knees, retrieving the twisty thing that he'd torn from her hair and tossed beneath the practice stairs platform. "Right now it looks as if I'll be sitting Amy down to tell her all of Morty's good points and convince her it's okay to go out with him. Just give me a call when your guests arrive, and we'll wing it."

He looked away from the tempting wiggle of that fanny in the air. Oh, yeah. Judging by the leap of interest beneath the towel, his body was ready to volunteer for the sexy makeover mission. But she'd wisely hesitated to accept that kind of repayment from him. Maybe he could content himself with some verbal tips.

His whole body seemed to sag with disappointment.

Tess—friend. Any other woman—lover. He chanted like a caveman in his head and made sure his hormones understood the distinction by the time she stood to say goodbye. Travis winked into her guileless hazel eyes and said the words a friend would want to hear. "For what it's worth, T-bone? Morty should've asked you out."

"MORTY SHOULD'VE asked you out."

Yeah, but Morty hadn't.

Tess had tried to get down and dirty with Travis, but that hadn't happened, either. For a few feverish minutes, she'd been someone else. Someone sexy. Someone *hot*, to quote Travis himself.

Tess wiped the fog from the mirror over the sink and wrapped the bath towel beneath her arms. She caught her breath as the terry cloth rubbed across her nipples in a rough caress and they jumped to life, just as they had beneath the rasp of Travis's tongue. A memory throbbed between her legs and she squeezed her thighs together. Her own hands went to her breast and waist, easing the torment of a body that remembered every touch that had left her on the brink of fulfillment, every kiss that had promised such pleasure, as if only seconds had passed instead of hours since Travis had pulled her onto that massage table with him.

That was how a man should make her feel.

That was what was missing from her life.

That rush, that fire, and the pay-off she'd denied herself today were things she deserved. There was only so much a girl could do with a towel and the handheld entertainment she kept in the table beside her bed.

She looked at the woman in the mirror—her wet hair plastered to her scalp, her face scrubbed of any makeup, her hand clutching her breast—and for one brief moment, Tess saw herself the way Travis said she should.

She was irresistible.

There were curves beneath that towel. Seduction in those drowsy eyes and parted lips and bold hand. And the heat that opened her pores and glazed a sheen of dampness across her tanned skin didn't come entirely from the shower she'd just taken.

No other man had ever made her feel this way. Had ever made her believe she was sexy.

But then she blinked and the plain brown mouse everyone else saw reappeared in the mirror. Ashton's future Nixa Newhaven. Reliable as Old Faithful and common as a mud pot. Just about as sexy, too. Glub. Glub.

Travis claimed he could save her from spinsterhood by changing her reputation in town. At least he could save her from involuntary celibacy. With a little guided practice from him, he'd force the men of Ashton to see her as an exciting, sexy, datable—bedable—woman. Maybe their interest in her could spark her desire for one of them.

Tess snorted at her silly reflection. Yeah. Woulda, coulda, shoulda.

The bald truth was she wanted Travis. *He* made her feel sexy without batting an eyelash. She didn't want to be made over for some other guy…but that was the practical thing to do, or else she'd be pining over Travis McCormick the rest of her life.

"Damn practicality." Why couldn't she just have what she wanted?

Why couldn't she?

Tess picked up her comb and started detangling the shoulder-length kinks of hair, along with her wandering thoughts. Nah, she couldn't. Could she?

He was home for two weeks. And then he'd be gone. They'd be reduced to e-mails and phone calls and letters. But for two weeks…?

"You shouldn't." She pointed to her reflection in the mirror. "But you want to."

Should she really trade in her best friend for a drill sergeant who could transform her into a lean, mean sex machine? What if Travis's so-called miracle makeover didn't take? Or what if it did and she discovered there wasn't another man in Ashton—or on the planet—she wanted as badly as she wanted him? Could she really walk away from a steamy, two-week training session like what they'd started on the massage table with her heart and pride and future intact?

Would a hot summer romance be enough to finally get him out of her system? Or would loving Travis forever spoil her for any other man?

Either she should ignore her attraction to Travis totally, or she should have the balls to see it through to its conclusion. She wasn't sure she was sophisticated enough to have it both ways. Sophisticated, right—that was probably on one of those *irresistible* genes she was missing.

"Make a decision, Bartlett." She frowned at the perplexed reflection in the mirror. "Go for it, or get over it."

"Who are you talking to?" Her comb clattered into the sink at the sharp rap on the bathroom door. Amy knocked on the door a second time. "Mom said dinner would be on the table in five."

Catching her startled breath, Tess retrieved her comb and returned it to her toiletry bag beside the sink. "I'll be there."

With her sister's knock, common sense returned. As did the memory of her promise to Morty.

"Hey, Ame—wait." Anchoring the towel with one hand, Tess opened the door before Amy bounced back down the stairs. "Got a minute?" She nodded toward her bedroom across the hall. "I need to talk to you."

Amy crossed her arms and regarded her with knowing brown eyes. "Need some sisterly advice?"

Tess opened the door and followed Amy into her room. "Not exactly."

"Then what, exactly, is going on?" Plopping on the end of the bed, Amy curled her legs beneath her and grinned. "You and Travis were gone a long time this afternoon. Make any headway on joining the two clans together?"

Tess turned to her dresser, hiding the self-conscious blush that stained her cheeks by digging out a pair of panties and a bra. "Travis and I were just…" Plain white cotton, she noted, designed for practicality and support. Would Travis's makeover include tossing out her underwear? Could the right bit of lace or color—or doing without—turn her into a seductress?

"You were what?" Amy shamelessly fished for a juicy tidbit.

Tess shoved the drawer shut and quickly pulled on the plain white turn-offs. "We were working out a training schedule."

"For two hours?"

Before her feverish cheeks revealed any more of her obsessive thoughts about the captain next door, Tess turned the conversation back to Amy. "I got a phone call, actually, that concerns you."

Amy caught the towel Tess threw at her. "Oh," she sighed in disappointment. "Oh!" She sat up straight and balled the wet towel against her chest. "It wasn't Barry, was it? The judge said I didn't have to speak to him anymore. God, it would be just like him to make a play for me now that I've made it clear I want nothing to do with him. I'll bet that cheesy little bimbette he was chasing doesn't look nearly so hot now that the thrill of cheating is—"

"No," Tess interrupted to reassure her sister and rescue the towel from her crushing grip. "I haven't heard from Barry the Butthead since your final hearing." Setting the towel safely out of harm's way, Tess sat beside Amy. "Morty Camden called. He said you met at the McCormicks' party on Thursday."

Amy exhaled an audible sigh of relief. "Oh, sure. Morty. Receding hairline. Glasses. He was in your class at school, wasn't he? He seemed older than that the other night. In a mature way, I mean. Not an old fogey. He has a lot of responsibility this week at the festival, doesn't he?"

"The Chamber of Commerce was lucky to have him volunteer for the festival committee this year. With him in charge of finances, nothing's gone over budget, and he's used his connections in the business community to get nearly everyone in Ashton involved." Was she laying it on too thick? Did Amy even realize how Tess was playing up Morty's good qualities?

"He's kind of quiet, but I imagine he's very responsible." Amy clapped her hands together and gasped in delight. "Did Morty ask you out? Go. You should go."

If she got this excited for her, then hopefully… "He wants to ask you out."

Amy's smile deflated. "On a date?"

"That's what they call 'em nowadays." Her sarcasm went unnoticed. Amy was up, pacing the room.

"I can't go on a date. I'm not ready for that."

"Your divorce was finalized in May. You were separated for months before that."

"Barry was the last man I dated. And I married him. I don't want to make that kind of mistake again."

"Relax. Morty isn't asking you to get married. He just wants to take you to the festival. Maybe dinner."

"Why didn't he ask me himself? What's wrong with him?" Amy clutched her pale cheeks. "What's wrong with me?"

"Nothing." Tess got up and wrapped firm hands around Amy's shoulders, shaking some calm into her sister. "Morty's a little shy, so I said I'd put in a good word for him. But he fully intends to call you later this evening. Looks like it's a good thing I mentioned it to you first so you won't wig out on him."

"I am not wigging out." Tess's unblinking stare told her another story. "Okay, maybe I am. Why would Morty want to go out with me?"

Tess released her sister to finish dressing. "Maybe because you're beautiful. He liked talking to you. He felt a connection that he'd like to explore a little bit further."

Amy was shaking her head. "But I'm an older woman."

"By three years," Tess scoffed. "Honey, you've got

to start seeing yourself in a new light. You are not Barry Friesen's neglected, put-upon wife anymore. You are a gorgeous blond career woman who deserves to have a little fun while she's home on vacation. It's time you ended this moping martyr routine and got on with your life. Summer's well underway. When are you going to start enjoying it?"

Chewing on a fingernail, her sister considered the advice. "Dating other men would be a good way to stick it to Barry."

"Now you're thinking." Tess slipped on her tennis shoes and urged Amy to the door. "An evening with Morty would be a safe, easy place to start. He might not be the most exciting man in town, but he's not a womanizer."

"That already puts him one up on Barry. And Morty's not that bad looking. If you look at him in a young Patrick Stewart with glasses kind of way, he's actually sort of cute. And you know what they say about bald men…" Amy halted abruptly. "Wait. You know what they say about bald men. Maybe you'd better come with us."

Tess groaned and shook her head. The man hadn't even asked her out yet and Amy was freaking. "I can't. I have to work the concession stand. Besides, three would definitely be a crowd in this case. Morty's looking for a real date with you, not just someone to fill up the other side of the seat on the ferris wheel."

"You think I should say yes?"

"It's just one date." And Tess had thought Amy was the Bartlett sister who had it all together when it came to men. "I've had a friendly lunch and dinner with Morty a few times, and he's sweet. A gentleman from the word go. Once you coax him out of his shell and get him talking about something he's knowledgeable on, he can be very interesting. And if you're bored to tears or you just don't click, you don't have to see him again. You're heading back to Richmond for school in a couple of weeks, anyway, so you can be up front about this not turning into any kind of relationship."

Amy started down the stairs to the kitchen. "I suppose. But it's scary, Tess. My skills are rusty. I was married for a lot of years. That means I haven't dated anyone since…" She paused on a step and turned, the frown line between her eyes indicating an unpleasant thought. No doubt something related to Barry.

"What?"

"Did I ever tell you about that summer in college when I was waitressing at The Bounty restaurant downtown?"

"Other than the fact it was the most money you'd ever made at a summer job and you hated that sailor outfit with the mini-skirt you had to wear, no, not much." Was Amy keeping secrets from her? "Why bring that up? That was before you met Barry, wasn't it?"

"The Bay Festival that year is probably what made Barry look so good." Amy's wry smile conveyed little humor. "Let's just say that my last date here in Ashton was an unqualified disaster. I sure can pick 'em."

Tess laid a reassuring hand on Amy's arm. "That was more than a decade ago. You're a different woman now. Don't put so much pressure on yourself."

"What if I haven't outgrown my knack for giving my heart to losers?"

"Morty might have retained a few of his nerdier qualities from high school, but I wouldn't call him a loser. And no one's asking you to fall in love. Just get out of the house and spend some time with the guy." Tess offered an encouraging smile. "I promise it'll be more fun than a root canal, and not nearly as painful."

"Oh, now you're really selling him to me." Amy's posture finally relaxed. "All right, I surrender. When Morty calls, I'll give it a shot. But if this date turns out to be as awful as my last festival date, I guarantee there won't be any second chances. I'll go for safe over hot any day."

"Safe?" Now Tess was the one frowning. That was the second mysterious reference Amy had made. "Did something happen that summer?"

Instead of answering, Amy chucked her under the chin. "It's just good to know that some things around here never change. Thanks for the pep talk, kiddo."

Amy waltzed off into the kitchen, leaving Tess alone with her troubling thoughts. She didn't know what bothered her more—the idea that Amy had gone through something heartbreaking without telling her, or the knowledge that even her own sister perceived her as one of those things around Ashton that never changed.

Tess had just spent five minutes convincing Amy to see herself in a new light. Maybe Tess needed to take her own advice and think a little less like that plain brown mouse and a little more like an irresistible woman.

6

TRAVIS STARED AT the screen on his laptop, drumming his fingers against his thigh as tension tightened inside him.

It was an e-mail from Clarksie in the Middle East.

Yo, Action Man.

Word travels a little slow over here, but I'm glad to hear the brass finally kicked you out of the hospital and made you go to work. 'Bout time you got off your duff. It's no fun playing jokes on the probies all by myself. That'd be sweet if you got reassigned to S.O. 6 when we're back stateside in a couple of weeks. When you make the cut again, the beer's on me.

You seen Becky lately? I know her job's taking her all over Virginia. I can't tell you how much it bites that I had to ship out before the honeymoon. Man, I miss her. Nobody here has hair that shade of blond. Not that I want you keeping her company. I know how you work the ladies, my friend. Still, it'd be nice to know somebody is keeping an eye on the Beckster for me.

Drop me a line sometime. I won't be able to check messages for a couple of days, but I'll be back. Count on it.

See you in two.

Clarksie

Travis clenched his jaw at the good natured teasing, meant to convey relief that he was in better shape than the last time Clarksie had seen him. He and Zachariah Clark, an overgrown farm boy from Nebraska, had known each other since basic. They'd secured plum assignments in Special Forces, had gone through weapons and ordinance school together, and had been Corps mates long enough to develop a bond that linked them across an ocean despite the miles of red tape that forced them to avoid any mention of a precise location or mission assignment.

But the urge to fire back the expected response—something terse and clever and teasingly graphic—couldn't get past the envy and guilt. Clarksie was overseas, doing his job. Taking the risks Travis should be taking. Living with the rats in his bunk and the sand in his boots that Travis should be living with. Putting his butt on the line because that's what their country had asked him to do.

Their country had asked Travis to go home and relax for four to six weeks. And if he wasn't careful, they'd hand him his discharge papers and pat him on the back and tell him his services were no longer needed. That he'd been replaced by a real man who could get the job done.

Yeah, that's what Clarksie wanted to hear. Him bitchin' and moanin' because he wasn't there with him.

Summoning a remnant of the old Captain McCormick, Travis flexed his fingers over the keyboard, took a deep breath and started to type.

Clarksie—

I know you're in the thick of it so I won't keep you.
I'm at home for a few days, resting up. My leg's good,
and the scars just make me prettier.

I told you there wouldn't be any rookie who could
take my place. Keep them in line or I'll have to come
over there to whip them into shape for you.

Yes, I saw Becky a couple of months back when
she stopped by the base. We went to lunch and
caught up. She's a regular Law & Order babe in that
pinstriped power suit. I tried to score some points,
but she shot me down. I swear, all we talked about
was you. "The big guy this, the big guy that." Should
I ask how you earned *that* nickname? Seriously, man.
She's tough. The state's attorney's office is getting
their money's worth with her. You take out the bad
guys there—she's locking them up over here. I'll give
her a call when I can to see if she needs anything.
But she's all yours. She misses you.

Keep your head down and watch your back since
I'm not there to do it for you.

See you in two.

Action Man

Travis read through his words carefully before
hitting *Send*. He'd told a few lies about the leg and the
flirting and told the man the truth he needed to hear
most about his wife's love. If Clarksie got a laugh or
two from the e-mail, as well as the morale boost of con-
necting with a voice from home, Travis would be happy.

If *he* could live up to the claims he'd made, Travis
would be even happier. He intended to be in his service

uniform and on hand to meet the plane when his former S.O. 6 unit landed stateside.

"Be safe, buddy." Travis patted the laptop, aching to be something more substantial than that voice from home. What if one of the new guys in the unit—the probies—missed a booby trap during a mine sweep? What if their rookie eyes overlooked a flash in the mountains that warned a veteran like him of a hostile's location? Hell, what if none of them could appreciate the twisted sense of humor that he and Clarksie shared? His unit needed him—for protection, guidance, and a good laugh.

Who was he kidding? Travis needed them.

The doorbell rang, pulling him from the downward spiral of his thoughts. As he closed his laptop, he could hear his dad answering the door. Ethan was there with a crisp military greeting, too. Then there were female voices and introductions all round.

Travis stood, smoothing out any wrinkles in his khaki slacks and making sure his navy-blue polo was neatly tucked inside his belt. If he could have worn a full-dress uniform to show General Craddock that he looked the part of an active duty Marine, he would have. But his beach-front best would have to do.

Before joining the others in the foyer, he slipped his fingers through the blinds of the guest room window and parted them far enough to see the second floor of the Bartlett house. The curtain moved at Tess's window and he knew she'd been watching for the general's arrival. Perfect.

A slow smile eased across his face. He drew his shoulders back, burying a flutter of anxiety beneath steely resolve.

Show time.

"General Craddock." Travis had his hand out in welcome as he strode down the hall to join their guests. He ignored the minor twinges in his joints and exchanged a firm handshake with the superior officer who could make his reinstatement to S.O. 6 happen. "Welcome, sir. Or should I be saluting you?"

The lines beside Craddock's eyes crinkled. "I already warned Ethan about that. For the next forty-eight hours we are all off the clock. In fact, I'll be taking orders from Hal, here, as soon as we get on that boat."

"You know I'd be outranking you, anyway, if I'd stayed in the Corps, Walter." Travis's father couldn't resist getting a gibe in on his lifelong friend. "Better get used to it."

Craddock touched his brow in a mock salute and grinned. "Yes, sir."

Travis turned to the petite, dark-haired woman standing beside the general. "Mrs. Craddock." He smiled in a way that never failed to charm women of all ages. "It's a pleasure to see you again."

She returned the smile with a knowing wink and a maternal scold. "At ease, Captain. And it's Millie. I'm off duty for a couple of days myself. No need to butter me up."

Travis raised his hands in surrender. "All right, all right. I'll have Dad put you to work, too. I suppose after being married to the general so long, you know how to take an order?"

"She knows how to give one, you mean," Craddock insisted, and every married or once-married Marine in the room laughed with a knowing nod.

"My job is to work on my tan and enjoy the ride—

and to have some sandwiches on hand in case these two old salts fail to catch anything." After a yammering of friendly put-downs and challenges and protests in defense of all things sacred when it came to the art of fishing, Millie gestured toward the slightly plump, fiftyish, auburn-haired woman lingering in the doorway. "Before we get too settled in, I thought Eileen and I could run to the store and stock up on some snacks."

"Oh, ye of little faith," Walter said in feigned offense. "I will provide. I promise." He clapped his hand over the redhead's shoulder and pulled her between himself and Millie. "We need to finish introductions. Eileen Ward—my secretary—this is Hal's younger son, Travis—another fine Marine."

"Is there any other kind?" Travis's remark got a response from everyone except Eileen. Maybe her bun was too tight. "It's a pleasure to meet you, Mrs. Ward."

"Thank you for having me." She shook his proffered hand with absent-minded distraction, then snapped her full attention to her boss. "General, I'd be happy to make the grocery run myself, if someone would give me directions."

"Forget the groceries, already," Hal insisted. "I'm prepared for every contingency on this cruise. It's not like I haven't done it before."

"Yes, I'm sure. But… You see…" After a couple of nervous starts, as if the words she'd been searching for had failed her, she turned her attention back to General Craddock. "I thought we were going to spend some time in town. I didn't realize we'd be out on the water so long."

"Just overnight," Hal informed her.

She glanced over her shoulder. Judging by her expression, that seemed to be one night too long for the woman. "You don't want to leave the office unmanned tomorrow. The reports—"

"—will still be there when we get back." Craddock waved aside her concerns. "I'd give you a medal for dedication if I could, but you're being ridiculous. Captain Black will be there Monday. He'll answer the phone and manage the filing until we get back." He patted Eileen's shoulder. "We're here to relax, remember?"

"Kyle filing?" She touched her fingers to her temple as if that answer gave her a headache. "All the more reason to head back to the city."

"Eileen, Kyle can alphabetize as well as you…"

The debate continued, but all Travis heard was the name. "Black?" He let his gaze slide with an ominous portent to his big brother. As the conversation buzzed around them, he whispered, "Kyle Black? The same guy who used to be your aide?"

Ethan nodded. "When I got promoted to Embassy Guard Training School C.O. at Quantico, Black moved up to work for the general."

Not even Ethan knew the history he and Kyle Black shared. Not all of it, at any rate. If Travis's file crossed Black's desk enroute to General Craddock, he knew there'd be a damn good chance his paperwork could get *misplaced* for a few days. Maybe long enough for S.O. 6 to find a new captain before he ever had a decent shot at his old job. Yeah, calculated and underhanded— that would be Black's style of revenge.

Ethan's gray-blue eyes narrowed. "Something wrong?"

Before anyone else picked up on his suspicions, Travis shook his head. "Nah. It just feels like a bad omen whenever that guy's name comes up."

"I know the feeling." Ethan reached for J.C. and pulled her to his side. Travis frowned. Had big brother had some kind of run-in with Kyle Black, too? And why the protective gesture with his wife? "I never could knock him for his efficiency and resourcefulness, but he's definitely a man with a hidden agenda."

A knock on the door sidelined Travis's curiosity to follow up on Kyle Black. His entire mood lightened instantly when he saw Tess's beaming smile through the screen door.

"I haven't missed the party, have I?"

At his father's urging, Tess opened the door and came inside. There was another round of introductions and then the whole group moved into the living room.

"Do you and Travis have plans this afternoon?" Hal asked.

"Sure do," Tess answered.

Even though it was a Sunday, she wore one of her uniform polo shirts with the hospital's logo over one proud breast. Nice touch. No one could doubt that he would continue to heal under her watch.

"We're finishing up some last-minute preparations for the festival. Without Travis's help, I won't be ready for the onslaught of tourists we're expecting." She gave Travis a wink that sent a dozen unexpected smiles skittering through his veins. "I warned you I was going to put you to work when you volunteered."

Now he wished he had. He wished this wasn't an act for his father and Craddock's benefit. Yeah, he'd enjoy spending some extra time with Tess while he was home this summer. He'd tote and carry whatever load she asked of him, repay her any way she asked—not just because his father had visibly relaxed since her arrival, but because *his* mood had improved upon seeing her.

He owed Tess for that.

He just wished that repayment could be something a little more enticing. Something that involved kissing and getting naked and full body contact instead of driving and hauling and unpacking a few boxes. Travis closed his eyes and silently chanted his current mantra: Tess—friend. Any other woman…

Hell. Now that the changes he'd seen in Tess filled his head, he was having a hard time thinking about any other woman. His eyes popped open to find her still standing among the circle of friends and family—still sexy, still smiling.

Travis swallowed hard. He'd better keep his focus on the masquerade at hand. He'd talked her into providing an alibi to relieve Hal's concerns and help him look good in front of General Craddock. The absolute least he could do was to play his part as well as she was playing hers.

"So much for my vacation." Laying a hand over his heart, Travis sighed. "Duty calls, I'm afraid. I can't ignore a damsel in distress, can I? You see why I have to bug out on the boat trip."

He made a point to glance toward General Craddock. Do you get it? This woman needed him to work—knew he was capable of hard work. She was counting on him to get the job done. The trust in Tess's voice and expression said he was a man that a woman, his community— even his country—could rely on.

But Craddock was focused on Tess. "I can see why he'd rather spend time with a pretty thing like you than a bunch of old farts like us."

"Pretty thing?" For an instant, confusion marred Tess's smiling facade.

Millie Craddock rescued Tess from the general's flirting. She nudged her husband in the shoulder. "Who are you calling an old fart, Walter Craddock? Speak for yourself. I intend to have a grand adventure out on the water."

Craddock dipped his chin and pressed a quick kiss to Millie's lips. "Honey, you will never be old. And I'll be right there beside you, having that adventure."

"That's the spirit." Hal slapped his friend on the back and grinned at Millie. "You keep this one in line, or we'll be tossing him overboard."

Everyone in the room laughed, except for Eileen, who'd perched stiffly on the edge of the sofa and was playing with the hem of her cotton sweater. "Just how adventurous are we going to be? I haven't been in a pool in years, much less the ocean."

"C'mon, Eileen." General Craddock eased himself onto the sofa beside her and tried to cajole his fretting assistant. "You told me you loved the water."

"To look at," she snapped. "To wade in." Then she visibly drew a breath to calm herself. She crossed her arms, smoothed a misplaced hair into her bun with shaky fingers. "I haven't been swimming since high school," she muttered under her breath, but in a voice loud enough for most of them to hear. "What if someone falls overboard?"

Poor woman. She likely didn't have anything against vacations. But she seemed a little shy. And she was definitely afraid of the water.

"That's why I insist everyone wears a life-jacket on

my boat." Hal propped his hands on his hips and looked down at Eileen as though it was his solemn duty as captain of the ship to reassure her personally. "That's why I run the weather-band constantly, so I know if there's a storm or choppy seas two days, two hours or even two minutes out. Besides, I've made this trip dozens of times. You'll be fine."

Was his father's chest puffing out? Or had he sucked in his stomach? Travis couldn't tell if Hal liked the woman or if he felt the need to defend old sea salts the world over.

"Don't worry." Hal leaned toward the doubting tilt of Eileen's chin. "If you fall into the water, we'll come back to get you."

Eileen's face blanched lily-white.

Ooh, Dad. Strike one. Never mention falling overboard to a woman afraid of the sea.

Time to move on before his father talked Eileen out of going and the trip got cancelled. He didn't need his dad standing guard over him, and he didn't want him moping around because he'd been cheated of his chance to fish.

Travis clapped his hands. "We've got an hour or so before Ethan and J.C. head back to Quantico and you sailors disembark to find the Great White Fish. How about I get everybody a cold drink. What'll you have?"

A chorus of responses followed him into the kitchen.

"I'll help," Tess volunteered.

Once he reached the relative privacy of the kitchen, Travis expelled a heavy breath. "It seems to be going well."

He pulled the bag of ice from the cooler on the counter and opened it, keeping one ear tuned to the hum of conversation in the living room, listening for any mention of him and his condition or job situation. He dumped the ice in the cooler.

Tess came up beside him, grabbed the empty plastic bag he'd tossed onto the counter and threw it into the trash. "Hmm. No brace, no limp. You must be hurtin'."

He tossed her a package of disposable plastic cups, which she caught like the error-free shortstop she'd always been. "Or I might just be feeling better."

"Overnight miracle cure, huh?" She undid the twist tie and pulled out a stack of cups.

She set the cups beside the cooler while he retrieved two beers and a pitcher of lemonade from the fridge. "Mind over body, that's all. And a damned determination to de-stress Dad's life and get *my* life back."

"I want you to kiss me again."

Every muscle inside Travis jerked in response. The pitcher clattered onto the counter, and if not for the lid, he'd have been wearing the contents. Travis steadied the pitcher and looked down at her over the jut of his shoulder to see if he'd really heard those words or just imagined them. The slight tremor in her fingertips as she lined the cups up in equidistant rows told him the invitation was for real. "Right now?"

After keeping everything cool, calm and collected in front of his dad and the general, the insistent hammering of his pulse now interfered with his ability to keep a coherent thought in his head. The only image that seemed to stick was the memory of Tess bending over the counter in *her* kitchen. This kitchen would do just as well. Knock the cups into the sink. Lift her onto the counter. Apparently, his body wanted to do a lot more than kiss.

But kissing was a place to start. Sidling close enough to feel the summer heat on her skin, he leaned in to grant her wish.

Tess braced her hand against his shoulder, pushed him back and denied him the pleasure. "Your father and two superior officers are just on the other side of that wall. I wasn't talking about doing it here."

"But you were talking about doing it." He pushed against the resistance of her hand, teasing her with the double entendre. "Who would have thought a good girl like you—"

"Travis. Your father—"

His father stormed into the kitchen.

"Did you get a load of that redhead? Talking about my boat and my skills like I'm some kind of amateur." Hal reached between Tess and Travis to grab one of the bottles of beer. He twisted off the cap and pitched it before downing a long, cold swallow.

"Problem, Dad?" he asked, watching Tess plunge her hands into the ice to fill the cups to their rims. Travis considered diving inside that cooler himself now that her surprising invitation had gotten his juices flowing.

Hal backed to the center of the kitchen and plopped his beer on the table. He raised his voice to a nasally, mocking pitch. "'Is there enough room on your ship?' 'How far out are we going?'" He pulled a tray of veggies and dip from the fridge and dropped his voice to its usual gruff tone. "What, does she think I'm taking her out in a row boat?"

"I doubt she means it personally, Dad."

"I'd bet money that Millie's trying to set me up with that woman. We have absolutely nothing in common.

Your mother would have trusted my judgment without questioning every word I say."

Ah, so Eileen Ward was suffering from an unfair comparison to Travis's beloved mother. Knowing how set in his ways Hal could be, Travis thought the woman deserved a break.

"Maybe she gets seasick," he speculated. "Or has an allergy to fish."

His father rolled his eyes and reached for his beer. "She acts like she has an allergy to me."

Tess stopped fiddling with the ice and reached for a tea towel while Hal drank past the halfway mark on his beer. "It sounds to me like Eileen hasn't been around the water much. Or else she's had a bad experience and tries to avoid it now. She said she wasn't much of a swimmer. Her reticence to get on the boat might have nothing to do with you or fishing."

Hal paused, frowning over the tilted neck of his beer bottle in a moment of subtle, yet genuine concern. "You mean like a phobia or something?"

"Possibly." She took the beer from his father's hand and replaced it with a glass of lemonade. Smooth move. "I'm sure she's nervous about meeting all of us. And how hard must it be to admit you're afraid of something in front of a bunch of strangers?"

"Don't write her off just yet, Dad." Travis picked up the tray, put a hand on his father's shoulder and walked him back toward the living room and their guests. "Give her a chance to fit in and relax."

"Relax? Ha. She's as uptight as that bun of hers." But his blue eyes softened as he shook his head. "That wasn't very charitable, was it? Maybe she doesn't know anything about boats. But I could teach her. I'd better give her a tour before we launch."

Tess came up on the opposite side and went up on tiptoe to kiss his father's cheek. "You're a kind man, Hal McCormick."

Hal dipped his head and returned the peck on the cheek. "Thanks, sweetie." Then he looked up at Travis and winked. "Keep an eye on this one, son."

"Yes, sir."

He did just that as soon as his father left the room. Blue eyes met those verdant gold beauties as Travis smiled down at Tess. She was better at calming his father than one of his blood pressure pills. Funny, she seemed to be having the opposite effect on Travis.

Since they stood so close to the archway and their guests could be in eavesdropping distance on the other side, Travis mouthed the words, "I want to kiss you, too."

Rosy color dotted Tess's cheeks before she turned back to the counter to finish pouring the lemonade. "I think he likes her."

Travis grinned and followed behind. She knew exactly what he'd said. Maybe she'd even guessed all the subtext behind that simple statement. "That'd be a real *Romeo and Juliet* scenario, wouldn't it? Dad falling for someone who can't stand fishing and life on the water."

"Eileen has certainly gotten his dander up. I haven't seen any woman in Ashton get under his skin like that. Not since your mom, of course. And it's been ten years since she passed away?"

Travis stopped right behind her, reaching around her for the unopened bottle of beer. He moved in close enough so that his thighs brushed against her bottom. The rounded temptation flinched, nudging against his groin, and a jolt of electricity winged through him as if it had been an intentionally seductive move. Picking up the beer without retreating an inch, he leaned in and whispered against her ear, "Tell me why you want to do this kissing thing again. I thought we decided that was weird."

Tess held herself perfectly still, as if avoiding actual contact would make the tension thrumming between them go away. "I had a chance to think more rationally at home. If it was weird, then we couldn't have gone that far. I don't know why the chemistry between us has changed, but—"

Her deep breath closed the centimeter between them, and the sudden brush of her citrus-scented hair against his chin made his own breath catch. He put the bottle back on the counter. Then he braced his hands on either side of her, gripping the edge of the sink to quell the carnal urges rocketing through him.

"—It's changed," he finished. He turned his nose and nuzzled her scent, unable to deny the lure that pumped heat into his veins. "It's like you grew up while I was away. Grew sexy."

"I don't want to jeopardize our friendship." She tried to hold herself still within the circle of his body, but her shallow breaths revealed that he wasn't the only one fighting to keep the libido in check. "But you said I could ask you for anything. I'm asking you for two weeks. I'm not happy with my life. I want something more. Something exciting. Something magical."

"For two weeks?" An affair with Tess would throw this forced R and R into an entirely different light.

"I know it's a cliché, but…when I think summer

romance, I think hot and fast. And then it's over and we move on. If we both go into this knowing it's just a temporary—"

Her words stuttered to a halt as he closed his teeth in a gentle nip at her earlobe. Then she turned her head, inviting his lips to graze at her temple and cross the velvety warmth of her cheek. She made that helpless noise of abandon in her throat and Travis moved his fingers there, feeling the vibration buzz through his skin and quicken his pulse.

"I'll give you hot and fast." He dragged his hand down the placket of her shirt, seeking more neutral territory. But he found the swell of her breast and palmed her instead.

Her purr became an outright moan. "We shouldn't… next dad…room…"

Man, he loved how her words got all tangled up when she was turned on.

"Stop… catch us…" She pleaded even as she twisted her bottom against him.

Travis groaned with the need to thrust against her. But some sixth sense warned him a split-second before they were discovered, and Travis leaned forward, trapping Tess against the sink and stilling the subtle gyrations of her body. "Shh," he whispered.

A woman's bright voice entered the kitchen behind them. "Do you two need any help with the drinks?"

He did the gallant thing, reaching around Tess to turn on the faucet, blocking Millie Craddock's view of the type of physical therapy he and Tess were practicing. "No. We've got it covered."

He noted how Tess looked down at her breast and

tensed. He had *her* covered. Okay, so maybe his efforts were just as self-indulgent as they were gallant. But unless Millie had X-ray vision, this would remain their own private therapy.

"You're sure?"

"Thanks, Millie. We just needed to clean up a little mess. We'll be out in a second."

"Great. Your dad is taking us down to the dock to give us a tour of his new boat."

Travis gently squeezed Tess's breast, catching the distended nipple in the crinkle of his palm. The running water masked her tortured sigh. His body masked the white-knuckled grasp she held on the edge of the sink. The blood surged through his veins. How could this woman be so responsive to the slightest touch? and not think she was sexy? The men of Ashton who hadn't noticed were either blind or stupid. And now they were going to be out of luck because he intended to be a very hands-on teacher.

For two weeks.

"What did he call it?" Millie asked.

"Call what?" Travis wondered how fiery Tess's skin was beneath the polo shirt. Wondered if she felt anywhere near as feverish as he did.

"The name of his boat."

Hell. Travis jerked his chin to the side, glancing at Millie from the corner of his eye. She hovered in the archway, seemingly unaware of how playing with Tess was playing with his control. Easing his grip on Tess, Travis dug deep to give Millie a coherent answer. "The Helena Two. After Mom."

"That's right. The first Helena was smaller. I

remember it from last summer." Millie hesitated, as though she might suspect that all was not as innocent as it should be in the kitchen. "Do you mind bringing the drinks to us down at the dock?"

"We'll deliver." Travis slid his hand to the flat of Tess's stomach.

"Are you sure?" Millie's voice drew closer. "I don't mind helping."

Tess leaned forward and shut off the water. "We've got it." She cleared her throat to mask the husky timbre of her voice, "We'll be right there."

"It's relaxing to not have to play hostess myself for a change. Thanks."

The instant Millie left, Tess snatched at Travis's hand. The moment the voices in the living room drifted outside and the back door slid shut behind them, she shoved Travis back and shot across to the other side of the room. "You're naughty. We can't do anything *here*. And we can't do it *now*." Travis followed her at a leisurely pace, stalking his quarry. He changed course when she darted toward a row of cabinets. She pulled out a plastic tray and set it on the counter, rambling on while she busied her hands with realigning the cups there. "I really do have to set up the concession stand for the festival this evening. But maybe we could schedule a time when you could give me some pointers."

"I'd love to give you a pointer."

He was right behind her when she turned. "Travis!" She swatted at his shoulder and ducked beneath his arm to head for the fridge. "What if Mrs. Craddock says something to your dad?"

Travis grinned at the blush on her cheeks, wondering how much of it was from embarrassment at nearly getting caught, and how much was due to the flirting and touching itself. "First of all, Millie's cool. Second, she didn't see anything she shouldn't. And third, if Dad did find out I could get it on with a woman in the kitchen, then he'd be a lot less worried about the state of my physical health."

When she closed the refrigerator door and turned, Travis trapped her there, backing her against the cold metal with a hand braced at either side of her waist. When he bent his head for the next kissing lesson, she shoved the pitcher of water against his chest, wedging a few inches between them. "Can you cool it for a second? I want to lay it on the line here. I know you have a lot more experience with sex and knowing what's sexy than I do. I want you to teach me a few techniques that will blow my tomboy-next-door image out of the water and transform me into that irresistible woman you talked about. I want this summer to be unforgettable."

If he wasn't a tough Marine, the icy condensation that soaked through his shirt and chilled his skin might have deterred him from making another pass at those rose-tinted lips. "Whatever you're doing right now works for me."

"Travis—"

"That's it," he whispered, nibbling at the swell of her lush bottom lip. "Keep saying my name. Over and over like you can't get enough of me."

"That's not what I meant."

"Isn't it?" He pried the pitcher from her grip, and his temperature started to rise again when she warmed the damp knit against his chest with her hands. Though sensing she was making no real effort to escape, he pressed his hips into hers, anchoring her to the spot while he set the water on the counter beside the fridge. "If we let this thing follow its natural course, you'll be moaning my name in that sexy voice you get when you're turned on. And just so we're clear—I fully intend to turn you on."

"Travis. Stop." Her voice quivered, falling far short of being stern with him.

"Yeah. Like that." He tunneled his fingers into her hair and freed the silky waves from its ponytail. "Like saying my name is a secret code for 'I want you'."

"Travis!"

"Oh, yeah, she wants me bad." He dipped his mouth and settled his lips squarely over hers.

Refrigerator magnets became casualties of the next few minutes of nipping and licking and kissing and fondling and driving himself mad with the craving to possess this woman right here, right now. He hooked his hand behind her knee and pulled her thigh up against his hip. His fingers tangled in her hair, and his tongue taught hers amazing, wicked things that she quickly learned and gave back in ways that made him question whether he had anything to teach her about sex and seduction.

And then, as cruelly and abruptly as dumping that pitcher of ice water over him, Tess tore her mouth from his. She pulled her arms from around his neck and hugged them across her stomach and chest. "I can't… we…here…" At least she had the balls to look him in the eye when she retreated. "I can't do this in your father's kitchen."

"Do *not* tell me this is weird, T-bone," he whispered

raggedly, resting his forehead against hers as he heaved to take in a calming breath of air. He let her foot slide to the floor and backed his swollen dick away from the tempting heat between her legs. "This is right. This is magic."

Her kiss-stained lips tried to smile around a stuttering sigh. But the clear articulation of her words told him the moment had passed. "This is crazy. You're a man of duty. You should understand. We have responsibilities. We can't just drop our pants and do it right now."

"Why not?"

Her breathy laugh was more of a sigh as she patted his chest. "Lemonade? Guests? Waiting for us?"

"Son of a bitch." He spread his hands wide and stepped back, breaking any last contact between them. This time, he left nothing to his imagination. He took the pitcher to the sink, poured the cold, clear liquid into his hands and doused his face. He washed the taste of her from his mouth and smoothed another chilly palmful over the back of his neck before he could face her again. "You know, it's not fair for you to be right *and* hot at the same time."

He'd gotten carried away. Pushed the moment too far too fast. He'd forgotten his whole purpose for inviting Tess over in the first place. Ensure the job. Placate Dad.

A year without sex had left him with some serious timing issues when it came to getting laid.

This would-be affair demanded patience. Planning. As she pulled her hair back into the confines of a practical ponytail, he remembered that Tess had a few doubts about her sexual image. Ones he couldn't fathom, but then, he couldn't get inside her head. Her erotic instincts were good, her desire for him obvious. But he needed to wait for her brain to get to the same place that her body was.

He could wait.

But there was nothing that said he couldn't speed up the process.

"Let's make a pact," he suggested, propping his hands at his hips and waiting for her to come to him. "The way we did when we were kids. You help me, I help you. You've got natural talent in the sex appeal department, T-bone. I'll help you showcase those talents in whatever way I can. I think your offer has to be the best damn way to spend a summer vacation that I've ever signed on for."

She tried to be businesslike, but failed adorably by clearing her throat—twice—before sticking out her hand to shake on the deal. "So we're agreed. In exchange for smoothing away your dad's worries and impressing General Craddock, you'll put me through some basic training."

He eyed the outstretched hand for a moment before taking it lightly in his grip. His gentle hold was more caress than handshake, but she didn't pull away. "Deal. As long as you understand where this is going, that we'll have two weeks to explore whatever it is you think you don't know, and that we won't have any regrets when we're done."

"We'll go back to being friends?"

"That's the deal. Say my name and tell me you understand."

"I understand."

"Say my name."

"I understand…Travis." Her throaty voice heated his blood all the way down to his toes.

He grinned. Kissed her hand. Promised her everything her eyes were asking of him. Promised himself. "I want you, too."

7

KYLE BLACK LURKED in the shadows across the street, munching his popcorn one precise kernel at a time and spying on the Chamber of Commerce concession booth. Or, more accurately, he studied the activity in and around the corrugated steel trailer.

The side door had been propped open and the front awning partially raised to encourage a breeze without giving the appearance of being open for business just yet. The lights inside spilled illumination onto the surrounding sidewalk and street, and gave him a clear view through the screened windows of the two women working inside. A man, whose buzz cut of hair pegged him as military, limped onto the curb, hauling soda canisters from the back of a pickup truck into the stand.

"How the mighty have fallen," Kyle whispered with a smile, slowly chewing a salty morsel. Captain Hotshot had been reduced to manual labor. His action days were over.

While McCormick's fall from the spotlight amused him, it wasn't enough to even the score.

The key to revenge lay in taking away what a man wanted most. And though he'd been diligently working in Washington, D.C., at the time of Travis McCormick's accident, he took a perverse personal pleasure in seeing that limp. Captain McCormick's personnel file had listed him in hospital for six months and on injured leave for three months after that. Then he'd been returned to light duty, stateside, pushing papers.

It was a fate worse than death for a hoo-yah hero like Travis McCormick.

Kyle had tracked down McCormick's request to be reinstated to Special Ops. He knew that some percentage of General Craddock's reason for visiting his old Marine Corps buddy this particular week was to see firsthand whether or not Travis could handle the physical demands and mental stress of Special Ops.

McCormick caught his foot on the curb, stumbled a step and swore. The heavy canisters smacked onto the concrete. For a moment, Travis leaned heavily on one, then plopped his butt down on top of it and massaged his leg around the elastic brace on his left knee while letting some colorful curses fly.

Laughter rumbled low in Kyle's throat.

Any sound he made was masked by the noises from downtown Ashton—a handful of cars passing by before Main Street would be blocked off at 5:00 a.m. for the festival, the twangy whines and soulful vocals of a country band doing a sound check at the courthouse stage, the drone of tourists and locals walking the historic district and hanging out at bars. The stealth was intentional. Kyle wasn't ready to be discovered. Not until he'd done a thorough recon of the situation and decided on the best course of action.

He popped another kernel into his mouth and processed what he'd learned thus far.

Travis McCormick's influential father, the man who'd demolished red tape to get his wounded son the best medical care on the continent, had set sail with General Craddock and company at precisely sixteen hundred hours that afternoon. Kyle's former boss, Ethan McCormick, had departed with his wife at 1630. Travis had lingered at the house another hour and a half before climbing into his father's truck and driving into town. After circling the main drag, he'd parked beside the concession stand, where a silver-haired lady had accepted a kiss on the cheek and then put him to work. That gray-hair was long gone, but—

"Crap." Kyle spat out the popcorn. Amy was there.

Her rejection burned as fresh as it had a decade ago.

And now she was fawning over McCormick.

Responding to his whining, Amy—a honey-gold blonde with stilts for legs and a body that should have belonged to him—ran out of the concession stand. Kyle's heart pounded in his breast. Nerves tingled and blood surged with remembered desire.

Amy's sister was there, too. Tess—a shorter, duller copy of her sister. She knelt in front of Travis, inspecting the knee while Amy hugged her arms around his shoulders. Both were concerned, supportive. Falling over themselves to offer aid and comfort to his enemy.

A lot of years had passed since he'd last visited Ashton, but not a lot had changed. *She* hadn't changed.

Kyle drifted forward half a step, remembering only at the last moment to pull back into the shadows between the two brick buildings.

For a few moments he was a younger man, fresh out of basic, out on the town with his buddies who'd survived

OTS, flirting with the local girls, having fun. He'd climbed the ferris wheel on a dare, then met a beautiful girl on the carousel and spent a long evening indulging in caramel apples, popcorn and kisses. He'd come back the second night, ditched his friends and found her again. Then the week was over and he shipped out with his unit.

Kyle wrote the girl, loved the girl, lost the girl.

And now the girl was tucked under Travis McCormick's right arm, with her sister tucked under his left. She smiled and laughed, allowing McCormick to kiss her temple.

Not again.

The desire in Kyle's veins boiled into something ugly. He wadded up what was left of the popcorn and tossed it behind him into the alley. Leaving his hiding place, he marched toward the street to tell McCormick to get his damn hands off Kyle's woman.

But a car pulled up to the curb, right in front of Kyle, forcing him back a step. The car was a boxy hybrid thing that screamed nerdy practicality. The four-eyed freak behind the wheel had nearly clipped him, and instead of apologizing, he rolled down the passenger-side window and called to the trio across the street.

"Hey, Tess. Travis. Amy."

"Damn." As McCormick and his harem turned, Kyle spun and fell into step behind a pair of sailors in town early for the festival. Observation and strategy were his strong suits. Any rash action now would only negate the plan forming in his head. At the first opportunity, he ducked into the shadows of a recessed store front and turned back to watch the nerd shake hands with Travis and Amy. He hugged Tess.

What the hell? McCormick had a new little buddy? Judging by the blushes and laughter, there was some teasing going on. Maybe some outright flirting between the men and women. Was McCormick teaching that runt how to steal a woman? Maybe he should start with how to get one in the first place.

Kyle could teach him a thing or two. He was every-thing a woman wanted: handsome, successful, a talented lover. Amy should have seen that. She never should have left him for McCormick that night. Should never have let McCormick turn her against him. Amy should have been his.

Wo-ho. What was that? Amy and the nerd went into the booth together. McCormick stayed outside with his arm around the younger sister, Tess Bartlett. He by-passed her temple and kissed her on the lips. But she blushed and shied away with a remark that made him laugh. He followed her toward the stand like a puppy trailing after a bone.

Travis McCormick was flirting with Tess, not Amy.

Kyle grinned at the notion, and it was enough to break his foul mood and allow rational thinking to kick in. He'd seen enough and knew what he had to do. He'd relish this mission.

After one last look, he cut through the next alleyway to the side street where he'd parked his Firebird. The details were falling into place. He knew just how to proceed. He owed the general a day at the DOD, but tomorrow night, he'd be back, and then he'd right a wrong that had haunted him for ten years.

That assignment to Special Ops wasn't the only thing he could take from Travis McCormick.

"ARE YOU SURE you're okay?" Tess asked, urging Travis toward the cooler holding open the concession stand door. But he refused to sit. He'd taken a dozen paces under his own steam, walking off the tingling effects of jarring his knee. She thought she'd sneak in some weight training by having him carry the heavy canisters. Her subtle form of physical therapy had gone without a hitch until that misstep on the curb. She thought he'd recovered just fine, but something was wrong. "Travis?"

Not a muscle yielded beneath her hands. He'd frozen, peering over her head into the darkness beyond the circle of streetlight where they stood outside the concession booth.

"Stay here with Amy and Morty."

It wasn't a request. He grasped her by the shoulders, shoved her inside the booth, then disappeared.

Goose bumps popped up across her skin as concern for his knee chilled into wary suspicion. Why had Travis suddenly gone on alert?

Tess glanced at her sister, holding a box of candy bars and patiently listening to Morty's account of the meeting he'd just come from. Amy couldn't get a word in edgewise, but she handed Morty a couple of candy bars and pointed. He got the hint to stack them on the display shelves behind the front counter, resuming his story while they worked. Deciding the two of them were safely occupied, Tess hurried after Travis.

She jogged across the street. The man was in full-blown Marine mode now, moving stealthily through the shadows and avoiding the pockets of light from the black iron street lamps. Though he seemed surprisingly light on his feet, despite the knee brace and string of curses she'd heard minutes ago, Tess caught up with him about half a block away. He'd paused at the corner of the alleyway between a craft shop and a fudgery. She slowed to sneak up behind him as he scanned the hazy pit of the alleyway.

"I thought I told you to stay put." Apparently her sneaking abilities needed some work.

At the warning rumble of his voice, she said, "I'm not one of your men. You can't give me an order like that. It scares me when you do."

With a shake of his head he took her hand and pulled her to him, angling his shoulder between her and the darkness as he stepped into the alley. "You couldn't take an order if you *were* a Marine. Has anyone ever used the term 'pigheaded' when describing you?"

Despite the teasing, Travis bristled with tension. This harder, edgier side of his personality thrilled her with its intensity, while the uncharacteristic seriousness of it made her uneasy. "What's wrong?"

He didn't mince words as he checked behind a stack of crates and pallets. "Someone was watching us. Watching the stand."

"It was probably just someone trying to figure out whether we were open or not."

"No. This felt personal. Malevolent." His grip tightened imperceptibly around hers. "A good soldier develops a sixth sense about the enemy's location."

"The enemy?" The bay was calm tonight, the ocean breeze nonexistent. Still, Tess shivered at the portent in his words. "You mean like terrorists? Criminals? Here in Ashton?"

Now she was searching, too, glancing over her shoulder at the car driving past, seeking the source of men's laughter passing by on the sidewalk. She wrapped her free hand around Travis's corded forearm and slid closer to his hardness and warmth as she identified the shapes in the shadows around her for herself. A fire escape. An old coal chute that had been sealed off. A cat on the prowl.

Normally, Ashton didn't have much of a crime rate. But with the huge influx of visitors this first week of July, incidents of vandalism, public drunkenness—even assault—occurred. Robbing the concession stand wouldn't be a far-fetched possibility.

Tess squeezed Travis's hand. "Do you think we should call the police?"

She'd picked up on the malevolence Travis had sensed. Or maybe it was her own imagination that made her heart race.

"No." Travis stopped. She heard the even rush of his breath releasing before he turned and laid a callused palm against her cheek. "I don't think anything. I'm out of practice. My radar's off. There's nothing here." He sounded almost disappointed. "Sorry if I spooked you."

Though she didn't quite buy the brightening of his voice or the reassuring brush of his fingers, she gladly followed him back toward the light.

That's when she spotted a wadded up ball of striped paper outside the fudgery's fire door. "Trav, wait." She pulled away and squatted down to get a closer look. She quickly identified it as a bag of popcorn. Fresh enough that she could still smell the butter. "Your radar's fine. Somebody *was* here."

"Yeah, somebody too lazy to find a trash can." He tugged her back to her feet. His white teeth flashed, reflecting the glow of the nearest wrought-iron light, but she couldn't see if his grin was real or a put-on for reassurance. "C'mon. Let's find out if Morty's worked up the nerve to ask Amy out yet."

"But—"

"There's no one here. There's no danger." He hooked his arm around her shoulders and headed toward the street. "Let's go practice being irresistible."

"What do you have in mind?" Tess asked, letting him change the topic.

"How about a little more of that kissing?" he answered, steering her onto the sidewalk and filling the air with possibilities.

The anticipation was almost enough to distract her from the tension in Travis's posture. Almost. Did he really want to initiate a training session? Or was the instant vibe simmering between them just a convenient excuse to keep her from worrying about popcorn-eating spies?

Though she found herself checking the shadows along the street as Travis's keen gaze darted from side to side, the promise of completing what he'd tried to start in his father's kitchen that afternoon tripped along her pulse and heated her from the inside out. Tess hadn't been ready then. It had been too much, too fast—and so perfect it had frightened her.

The man could kiss. He knew the nuances of secret touches and bold risks and teasing words, and how they could seduce a woman. But having the sophistication to steal an erotic moment with Travis in his father's kitchen with an audience so close at hand must come with the femme fatale chromosome that Tess lacked. One yelp of ecstasy from her mouth and they'd have been interrupted by Hal, General Craddock and the rest of the bunch. Not exactly the sort of attention she'd hoped to gain.

Besides, she'd taken an awfully big risk just suggesting an affair. Her confidence had a little catching up to do with her desire. She wanted Travis. That hadn't changed. And as she walked along, pressed against his lean, solid flank and breathing in his musky, clean scent, that want only intensified. They'd walked down the street like this a dozen times before—his arm looped around her shoulders, her thumb hooked into a belt loop at his waist. But this time it was more than a friendly stroll away from a bar or a movie—this time, it was leading to something intimate, something new. A place where her body yearned to go.

But she needed to take this slowly. She wanted to make sure that she could deliver enough satisfaction so that Travis could enjoy teaching her just as much as she enjoyed learning. And she needed to do it without complicating the two-week time limit by mistaking a healthy, adult summer escape for anything deeper between them.

It was the least one friend could do for another.

She leaned into his side as she felt him relax, glad they were taking the long way down to the corner before crossing the street. They needed a moment to talk before rejoining Morty and Amy. "Did you want to go to your house? Or maybe see how far back we can push the seats in my car?" she suggested. "I have to stay here until the concession stand is good to go, but I know a country road that doesn't get traffic late at night. When we're done here, we could go there and play in the dark for a while."

"Play in the dark?" Travis scoffed, squinching his handsome face into a chastizing frown. "Are you afraid to show off your sexy side, T-bone? I want to see you—and hear you—when you come for me."

Tess sputtered. "I'm not afraid, I'm just being practical."

He stopped in his tracks and Tess stumbled forward. But Travis's strong arms caught her and turned her, scooping her up against him. He dipped his head and his wicked smile brushed against her cheek as he murmured in her ear, "I dare you to do something with me right here. Right now." His voice dropped to a bone-deep pitch that hummed along her nerves like a physical caress. The hand at her back slipped down to her backside. "Just like you dared me to kiss you at the hospital."

"Technically, I never in so many words—"

He squeezed her butt and lifted, rubbing his chest into her breasts with a slow, deliberate friction. Her nipples popped to attention, and the heat stoked by the pressure on her achy tips seared away her ability to speak.

"You have to learn to understand what you're saying even when there aren't any words." He nuzzled her cheek, then traced the shell of her ear with his moist, raspy tongue, making her shiver. "That was a dare, and you know it. Just like in Dad's kitchen this afternoon. I believe your exact words were, 'I want you to kiss me again.'"

His mouth hovered close enough to hers that the damp warmth of his breath brushed across her lips. They quivered, parting in response. For a few seconds the world lost all logic and she was leaning in, giving in. But a garble of indistinct voices joking and laughing somewhere in the distance pierced the haze of unfiltered desire and touched that one last rational brain cell.

The slight tensing she felt in the muscles across Travis's chest and arms told her that he'd heard them, too.

A second brain cell kicked in and Tess reached for his hand and moved it to a more neutral position at her waist. Without protest, he let her slide back to the pavement and gain a few inches of sanity between them. "I do want you to kiss me again, and let that kiss take us wherever we want to go." She fingered the neckline of his T-shirt and smoothed it across his skin. "But I didn't want my first time with you to be in front of an audience. Your dad has a heart condition, remember? I don't think catching us on the kitchen floor would do much to convince him that I'm taking care of you while he's gone."

He rubbed his hands up and down her back. His eyes shadowed with a uniquely Travis mixture of suggestion and regret. "I bet I could show you how to take very good care of me."

She fisted her hand and tapped it against his shoulder in a gentle reprimand for his ceaseless flirting. "Travis."

"Is that the, 'I want you, Travis' or the, 'No way, no how, not in the middle of Main Street, Travis'?"

Tess laughed, relieved that he wasn't angry with her. "Both."

"All right." He planted a teasingly chaste kiss on her mouth, then pulled away, capturing her hand and pulling her into step beside him. "If you're gonna go all smart and sensible on me, then we'll wait. I'm a patient man."

"Since when?"

He grunted half a laugh, giving her that one. "You want a lesson in being irresistible? Just keep in mind that one of the things a man is most attracted to is that sense of surprise. That…" he gestured in the air, trying to find the right words, "you-never-know-when-or-where-it-might-happen anticipation. Like, you want him so bad, you don't know if you'll be able to hold back and be discreet every time. That's a signal a man can't miss."

A woman couldn't miss that kind of signal, either. Tess swallowed hard. That was exactly how he made *her* feel. That unpredictability, backed up by the security of knowing he was a man she could trust, was one of the traits that made him so downright appealing.

That was exactly the kind of thing she wanted to experiment with. Varying her routine would certainly spice up her life. Or her summer, at least. She needed to toss aside the smart and sensible Tess Bartlett every now and then. She needed to quit thinking so much. Quit being so predictable. So reliable.

She squeezed Travis's hand, thanking him, promising him. "Who knows? I might surprise you."

"You've been full of surprises since I came home. Believe me, I'll be waiting for that—" Two men zipped around the corner of the last building. Travis jerked her back to save her from being plowed over. "Whoa."

The two well-honed twenty-somethings in jeans and crew-cuts were just as startled as she. And while they raised apologetic hands and backed away, Travis's grip on her wrist was tight enough to keep her anchored firmly behind him.

"Watch where you're going," he warned.

"Sorry, ma'am," the taller of the two answered. "Sir." Did his heels just click together? It was hard to tell with tennis shoes.

It was hard to feel any threat, either, when she saw them scrambling to decide whether to stop and chat or hurry their butts on out of there. She peeked around Travis's shoulder and offered them a smile. "Good evening."

"Evening, ma'am." The shorter of the two visibly relaxed at her greeting. "Hey, can you point us toward the nearest bar?"

Travis's hold finally eased, but instead of releasing her, he dropped his arm around her and pulled her to his side, needlessly staking a proprietary claim.

"The Bounty." Travis thumbed over his shoulder toward the intersection behind them. "Take a left on Fairfax. They serve drinks until one."

"Thank you, sir."

Even in cut-offs and a T-shirt, Travis's military bearing must be evident to these young men. The taller one touched his fingers to his eyebrow and echoed his buddy. "Thank you, sir."

The shorter one thumped him on the back of the head. "You don't have to salute him, Thibbs. We're all off duty here. Right, sir?"

The familiar humor returned to Travis's voice, though he barely cracked a smile. "You boys old enough to drink?"

The taller man massaged the back of his neck. "I'm twenty-one, sir."

"Twenty-two," the other one chimed in.

Travis acknowledged their answers with a nod, then tacked on a second question that put Tess on guard again. "Either of you see anyone loitering around this block?"

The two young men exchanged looks, then shrugged. "No, sir."

"There you go with the 'sir' again." The fractionally older of the pair pulled his shoulders back and endeavored to look as mature and on the ball as Travis seemed to demand of them. "We just drove in from Camp LeJeune, but we'll keep our eyes open for anything that doesn't seem right."

"Be careful," Travis warned. But his eyes glittered with the message that they should still have fun. "Dismissed."

"Yes, sir," the shorter young man answered, then cringed as the other one swatted him and laughed. They split and circled around Tess and Travis, heading toward The Bounty.

"Was I ever that young?" Travis commented, glancing up and down the street before stepping off the curb.

But Tess wasn't in the mood for reminiscing. "You're still worried about that guy you think was watching the stand."

"I just don't like unanswered questions." Like the Travis of their youth, he chucked her under her chin, dismissing her concern. The reversion to safer, simpler interaction between them only worried her more. Something about this evening was bugging Travis, and for once, she didn't think it had anything to do with his injury. "We'd better hustle back. I hear raised voices from inside the stand."

Tess registered Amy's shouts and grumbles. "Oh, my God. I've never heard Morty argue with anybody."

Tess dashed up to the door, leaving Travis in her wake. "Amy?"

By the time she ducked into the stand, Tess determined there was only one raised voice. Amy paced back and forth between the display racks and popcorn machine, pressing her cell phone to her ear. Morty stood at the counter, holding a stack of candy boxes, his eyes wide behind his glasses. Tess spared him a sympathetic glance. She recognized the frustrated anger on her sister's red cheeks.

"What do I care if your girlfriend dumped you? Call someone in your little black book, not me."

"Barry?" Tess mouthed the question.

Amy nodded. "Then scratch my name out!"

Morty leaned over his boxes and whispered, "I believe 'Butthead' was the name she used."

"No doubt." While Tess didn't envy her sister dealing with an ex who was more interested in her after the divorce than during the marriage, she breathed a little easier knowing that sweet ol' Morty wasn't bearing the brunt of Amy's temper. "Did you ask her yet?"

Morty rolled his eyes toward her still-irate sister. "I was trying to when he called."

"Don't give up."

"When are you going to grow up? You can't always have what you want." Amy continued venting. "Are you kidding me? No. Do not come to town. Do not—" Barry must have hung up. Amy shook the phone in her fist. "Oh…you…" She dumped the device into the nacho cheese dispenser and clamped the lid shut. "Bastard!"

Travis's clean musky scent reached Tess an instant before he whispered from the doorway behind her shoulder. "I take it that's the ex?"

Tess nodded.

Amy was wired now, leaving no opportunity for questions or sympathy. She grabbed her purse and stormed toward the door. "Do you mind if I take off? If

I get home now, I can trample Barry's memory beneath my feet for an hour on the treadmill so I can relax enough to sleep."

"Can I offer you a lift home?" Morty dropped the boxes onto the counter and hurried after her.

"No, I don't need some man—"

"Amy." Tess cut her sister off before Morty unfairly took a lashing meant for Barry. "It's a practical solution. I can't leave until we're set up, and you can't take the car until I get everything unloaded from the trunk."

Amy tossed her golden hair behind her back and huffed, still managing to look gorgeous despite her anger. Tess suspected her desire to escape stemmed from a fear that she might break down and cry in front of an audience. But her sense of duty was still intact. "I shouldn't leave you alone. It's nearly midnight."

Travis leaned in, close enough for Tess to feel his body heat at her back. "I'll be here."

Amy looked over Tess's shoulder at him. Then she turned to Morty and sighed. "She's in good hands, then. All right, Morty. Drive me home."

Tess tried not to notice Morty taking a deep breath and steeling his shoulders as he and Amy slipped past them and headed for his car at the curb. She turned her face to the door frame to hide her amusement. Oh, he was going to need every bit of backbone he could muster to deal with Amy when she was in crush-Barry mode.

Fortunately, he'd gotten most of his talking done before the phone call because Amy was still on a tear as she climbed into the passenger seat. "You're not seeing anyone else right now, are you?"

"Me? No. I—"

"Good. I can't stand a cheating man, even if he's just a chauffeur…"

Tess and Travis watched the odd couple until they pulled away.

"Do you think Morty stands a chance?" Travis speculated.

"If he's patient. Pretty much all he can do is listen right now. But he's good at that."

"If you ask me, he just needs to haul off and kiss her. Startle her out of her obsession with her ex and get her thinking about the present. She's moved on before when a relationship tanked. She needs to do it again."

"Again?" Tess frowned. Was he referring to the summer she'd spent with his big brother? Hadn't Amy indicated that that had ended in a mutual parting of the ways without hard feelings on either side? "What are you talking about?"

Travis blinked his blue eyes and revealed nothing. "I'm just saying that she's a strong woman. She needs to get over the Butthead and give a better man a chance."

"Like Morty."

"Sure. Why not?" She could tell by the quick way he strode outside to retrieve the last two soda canisters that there was something more to his explanation that he was leaving out.

But she didn't push for any clarification. She was having a hard enough time figuring out how to move on with her own life. That was a man's way of thinking, Tess supposed—the Action Man's, to be precise. Just do it. Don't analyze, don't worry—take action. That philosophy was probably what made Travis so impatient to get back to his unit at the Corps. He'd had a year to do too much thinking and was ready to simply do.

In how many ways since they'd struck their deal had Travis advised her to adopt a little of that philosophy, too?

As the summer night cooled, Tess went back to work stacking boxes and cleaning up for tomorrow's opening. Travis soon rejoined her in the tiny building to hook up the hoses for the soda pop machine. They worked in a familiar, companionable silence, pushing aside thoughts of men lurking in shadows, injured legs and needy sisters. But the friendly ambiance that normally settled between them was charged with possibilities.

The small confines of the metal building filled with the evocative scents of chocolate and popcorn and Travis. An accidental brush of elbows raised goose bumps along her arm. A muffled curse over a pinched finger linked their gazes in a silent query and a wink of apology. As they used up the oxygen in the tiny space, the temperature seemed to rise, heated by the awareness blossoming inside Tess's body.

When the box she was putting away on the top shelf slipped, Travis darted behind her to reach up and catch it. With his long, hard torso stretched against her back and his thighs pushing her hips into the counter, she was trapped between the immovable object and his irresistible body.

When she felt his ragged gasp across the nape of her neck and she heard her own moan of need in her throat, Tess knew. It was time to stop thinking about how sexless her life was, and simply start being sexy.

Don't think. Just do.

"I think we've done all we can here tonight." But she didn't really mean it. A plan was forming. But she didn't want to put too much thought into it. Before she allowed internal critiques like risky, or it's too late, or you'll scream and wake the sheriff to enter her head, she asked, "Would you mind going out front to close the awning and lock it down?"

He cleared his throat and stepped away. "Sure, boss." He ambled out the door in that controlled stride of his. "No problem," he muttered. "No problem at all."

She felt the whoosh of air as the awning swung against the screens and blocked out the lights and sounds from the street. She heard the thunks and clicks of dead-bolts and padlocks. And when Travis strolled back in without noticing her behind the door, she saw the chance to prove that she could be everything he claimed she was.

"T-bone?" He reached the opposite wall and turned, frowning.

Tess gently pushed the door shut, stepping out from her hiding place. She slid the dead-bolt into place and locked them inside. Together. Alone.

She faced him again, pressing her back into the door's cool wood.

"Travis." I want you.

She waited for him to understand, to get the message she was trying to send. He went still for a moment. His eyes narrowed. And then he grinned.

All she said was, "Surprise."

8

TESS SHIVERED AGAINST the door as Travis took his damn sweet time closing the distance between them. He had a look of no turning back in his eyes, and the promise of making it worth her while in every deliberate step.

He braced one then the other hand against the door on either side of her face and leaned in. "I told you a man likes surprises."

His deep voice feathered against her eardrum as he dipped his nose close to her temple and slowly inhaled, as if savoring a delicious aroma. Tess lifted her cheek, thinking if she offered, he might kiss her there. But he quickly shifted his attention to the other temple and breathed deeply again.

"Travis." She reached up and tickled her palms against the golden shadow of his nighttime stubble.

But when she tried to angle his lips down for a kiss, he snatched her wrists and pinned them against the door above her head. "Uh-uh." His warm grip was gentle, but there was no budging from her vulnerable position. "I know you want me." His blue eyes hooded and focused on her mouth, caressing her lips without a single touch. Something deep inside Tess's belly steeped with a languid heat. "The feeling's mutual, believe me."

Travis leaned into his hands at her wrists, bringing his body close enough that she could arch her back and press against him if she wanted. But she was discovering a secret thrill in the wanting and waiting. The almost, but not quite. She didn't force contact, but couldn't help twisting her body restlessly.

"What do you want me to do?" She was both pupil seeking guidance and seductress teasing him with possibilities.

He lowered his mouth to the juncture of her neck and shoulder. Then he nipped the collar of her baseball shirt between his teeth and tugged it aside, exposing her skin to his heated breath without touching it. "Tell me exactly what's going on here," he demanded. She smelled the citrusy shampoo that clung to his hair as he bent even lower and did something with his lips and tongue to release the top button of her jersey. "I need to know right now if you're going to turn all smart and sensible again."

"This is that…" She squeezed her eyes shut but she could still feel his breath between her. "…want…" Tugging against his grip, she stretched her neck and turned her head to deny him even accidental contact as he moved back toward her mouth. "…so bad…" His body heat was scorching her, robbing her of coherent speech, and he hadn't even touched her yet! "…can't wait." His warm breath danced across her lips. Her tongue darted out to moisten them. "Discreet…n…" He blew a deliberate stream of air across her damp mouth and she jerked in response. "Not." The breath rushed out of her chest, "Travis." Her eyes popped open. "I want you now," she begged before words failed her again.

And then he kissed her. He skipped right past sweet and tender and ground his mouth against hers, driving his tongue inside and pouring accelerant on the flame that not touching had already kindled inside her.

He pushed his hard thighs into her hips, pinning her against the door and giving the thick, liquid heat gathering inside her no place to go but to build in intensity. Adjusting his grip on her wrists, he anchored her with one hand. The other brushed down the side of her neck, traced her sternum, boldly squeezed one heavy, aching breast, and then hooked its way down the front of her jersey, casting aside buttons one by one.

He stroked the rim of her lips with his tongue, then thrust inside to tangle with hers again. She tasted raw, potent heat. And while he feasted on her as if her kisses were a decadent treat, his hand had found bare, burning skin to palm and squeeze. Her stomach, her flank, her back. Then somehow her bra was loose and her breast was in his hand.

The blood in her veins boiled and rushed to every point of contact. Her rock-hard nipple. Her hungry mouth. The weeping center between her thighs. The heat pooled and swelled and erupted in a guttural moan deep in her throat.

Drawn by the sound, Travis shifted his assault and laved his tongue along the length of her throat. She could feel his penis bulging beneath his shorts and rubbing against her hip. Yes, he wanted her, too.

"I… Please…" Tess's voice came in breathless gasps and made no sense. She'd never been this aroused, this needy, before—never felt so close to losing control of that last, rational thought. She only knew she wanted to touch him. She wanted the one thing he was denying her. If she couldn't touch, couldn't give, couldn't find release, she'd bust right here against this door.

When his wet mouth closed over her breast and he swirled his tongue around her rigid peak, Tess screamed.

She clamped her mouth shut and he laughed in his throat. Another shout like that and someone would be calling the police, knocking on the door. But she couldn't find a voice to protest.

"Irresistible," he murmured against her skin, making a wet path to the other breast with his tongue.

Tess clenched her teeth and moaned. He knew how he was tormenting her. He wanted her to lose control.

She tugged at his grip and squirmed against his wicked mouth and unyielding chest.

His answer was to pop the snap on her shorts and lower the zipper. Tess nearly screamed again at just the thought of what he was about to do. "Long time…" she rasped, as he slipped his hand inside and reached around to squeeze her bottom. She tried to explain her limited experience, that she had *never* experienced anything like this. "For me…not…" He slid her shorts down to her ankles, "like…" he pulled at her knee, freeing one foot from the denim, "this…"

When he allowed her foot to touch the concrete floor again, he'd veed her legs apart and wedged his braced knee in between. "I love it when you can't talk."

He was kissing her again before she could argue that *he* was the reason she couldn't form a coherent sentence. She was squeezing her legs around his sturdy, sinewy thigh before she could say that his kisses were the only ones that made her babble.

His hand was palming the heavy, swollen heat between her thighs before she could confess that he'd kissed her like this once before, when he'd been heart-broken and drunk, and had passed out on her couch before he could finish what he'd begun. He, thank God, had never remembered how close they'd come to altering their friendship forever.

Tess could never forget.

Now, tonight, she was ready to alter the course of her life. Over the years, she'd stagnated, faded, never been complete. She'd allowed herself to become a sexless creature, stuck in a routine. Hiding her passions, dreams and desires. But for two weeks, with Travis, she was going to live like the woman she'd always wanted to be.

Summoning a burst of strength, Tess tried once more to free her wrists from his controlling grasp. But his grip only tightened. He pulled his mouth from hers and demanded that she look him in the eye as he pulled aside the soaked crotch of her panties and moistened his finger along her slick, swollen clit.

The pooling heat inside her bubbled up like a volcano about to erupt. She was going to come. She had no control.

He slid one finger inside her, then two. Tess's breaths mingled with the moans in her throat, but she refused to look away.

Then, at the same time that he twirled his fingers, he pressed his thumb to that most tender spot. Tess bucked against his hand, struggling to breathe, trapped in his gaze. He rubbed her, worked her, inside and out, until she had to beg, "Travis... Trav..."

"Is that the 'Travis, I want you,' or 'Travis, do me now'?"

"Dammit, Travis—"

She hadn't realized how weak her knees were until he released her. But as she wound her arms around his neck and sagged against him, he lifted her, peeling off her panties and leaving her shorts behind on the floor as he set her on the counter. The cool surface shocked her skin, but it was the only respite he gave her before he pulled her bottom to the edge of the counter and knelt between her legs.

"Trav—" She didn't know whether to clutch at the bronzed head of hair that contrasted with her own darker thatch, or reach back and cling to the frame of the screen behind her. "I don't know what… I never…"

"Easy." His strong fingers gently dug into her thighs as he spread her open. "Don't try to talk." His words vibrated against her slick, throbbing crevice. "Just let it happen."

The scent of her own excitement wafted up between them in a heady reminder of the passion she was capable of if given the chance. She gripped the edge of the counter as he pressed against her with his thumbs. She couldn't last. She was going to fly apart. He parted her folds. She gasped.

"Easy," he coaxed her.

"Just do it," she pleaded. "Just—"

And then that tongue that had done such amazing things to her mouth was inside her.

Tess yelped at the bolt of white-hot pleasure that shot through her. She slapped her hand to her mouth, lost her balance and tilted to the side.

Travis palmed her hip to help her sit up. He guided her hands back to the edge of the counter. He reached for the shelf behind him. "Don't quit on me now."

"It's embarrassing."

"It's hot."

She heard something rip. "But—"

He silenced her protest by sticking a candy bar in her mouth. "Hold on."

Chocolate. With caramel. And a sweet, chewy…

Tess screamed around the delectable treat as Travis licked her very core. With his lips surrounding his teeth to protect her, he nibbled at her swollen mound. He thrust his tongue inside and withdrew. Thrust again. And again.

Every nerve ending that she thought could take no more throbbed to life again. Fiery sensations built in every extremity—her fingertips, her toes, her taut, beaded nipples—and flowed to her core, moving faster and faster with every nip of his teeth and thrust of his tongue.

Her vocal cords hummed and the sound rose into her mouth.

Like sparks following a trail of gunpowder to its source, the pressure inside her converged in one spot.

Travis thrust his tongue inside her and she exploded.

Lights flashed behind her eyes as her release consumed her. Chocolate and caramel muffled her ecstatic scream. Then slowly, slowly, Tess remembered how to breathe. She thought to chew and swallow. She collapsed back against the screen frame and opened her eyes to find Travis standing between her legs, wearing a most satisfied grin.

He bit off the half of the candy bar still hanging from her mouth. "You're even sweeter."

Tess smoothed her hair back from her damp forehead. Somewhere along the line it had fallen loose from its ponytail. If she wasn't so tired, she'd laugh with delight. Or embarrassment. "I never knew I was so…"

Travis grinned and swallowed his bite of candy.

"Good ol' reliable Tess is a screamer. Do you have any idea how that would shock Nixa Newhaven?"

Latching on to the front of Travis's T-shirt, Tess sat up. "If Nixa ever orgasmed like that, she'd be screaming, too."

Travis's gaze dropped down between them. "I don't know. If Nixa ever looked like this, I might be tempted to coach her, too."

"You rat." Tess laughed. "You'd give her a heart attack."

But as she followed Travis's wondering eyes, she knew that seventy-something Nixa would never let herself be so shockingly displayed. Like a special candy, Tess sat on the edge of the counter with her shirt hanging open, her naked breasts poking from beneath her hanging bra, her legs shamelessly parted as she cooled and recovered from that sensual high.

Yet it wasn't her own immodest exhibition that shamed her into a blush from her head to her toes.

It was the distinctly awkward bulge she saw straining behind the zipper of Travis's shorts.

"Oh, my." She shoved him back a step, ignoring his questioning gaze as she hopped off the counter. "We're not done."

A tingling of anticipation coursed through her. After sparing a few moments to re-fasten her bra and hook a button on her Bosox jersey, Tess ignored the panties and shorts that Travis had retrieved. She pushed aside his outstretched hands to lift his shirt and unsnap his cut-offs.

"Whoa, T-bone. What are you doing?" He pushed her to arm's length.

But he didn't hang on so Tess twisted away and went down on her knees in front of him. With the gentlest of care she unzipped the denim and peeled it away from the jutting protusion in his boxer-briefs. Then she spread her hands over his taut, flat stomach and slipped her fingers beneath the elastic waistband.

His breath hissed above her and her clothes hit the floor beside her. This time, his hands wrapped around her upper arms, good and tight, and pulled her to her feet. He was smiling, with gritted teeth as he looked down into her eyes. "Honey, you can't do me. I don't have any protection. I just wanted you to know how sexy you are. How irresistible."

"Bull. You never could lie to me."

He tried to back away, but now she had *him* cornered. When his butt hit the counter and stalled his retreat, she pulled the elastic down and freed him. His penis jutted forward, a sleek, pulsing thing that bobbed with a need she wouldn't deny him.

She wrapped her hand around him, held on as he jerked within her grasp. Safety measures accounted for. They didn't have to trade bodily fluids to trade pleasures. He wanted this. Maybe as much as she suddenly did.

Tess slid her hand along his shaft until she met his groin. She let one curious finger stroke the sensitive skin underneath. He dug his fingers into her shoulders, holding on, not pushing away. Tess smiled. "I was supposed to be seducing you, anyway."

"Oh, you did, baby. Believe me, you…" His words ended in a strangled gasp.

"What's that?" Tess kept squeezing, rubbing, teasing, enjoying the power she now held over *her* helpless captor. His compliment gave her a confidence that made her bold. This was so not the same-old, same-old of her normal, predictable life. "The charming Captain Mc-Cormick has lost the ability to speak?"

"You're cruel."

Wrapping her free hand behind his neck, she pulled him down for a kiss. "No. I'm irresistible."

WAS SHE A different woman?

Or was he a different man?

Travis followed Tess to her car well after one in the morning, replaying the hour they'd just spent together. He'd been a happy man *before* she'd insisted on the hand job. What happened after that was just icing on the cake. No woman could fake what Tess had done. Even without the gibberish and screams, her body had given her away. Any man would feel like a mighty potent son-of-a-gun if he could make a woman come like that.

Travis hadn't felt a rush like that for a long time. A year, to be exact. But locked inside the concession stand for an hour with Tess, he'd felt powerful. Whole. He'd been Captain Travis McCormick again, decorated Marine.

He'd been a man.

Upon his homecoming, he'd turned to Tess for the normalcy of a familiar friendship. He'd quickly shot *normal* out of the water with his cranky reaction to her insistence on lengthy physical therapy. And then, when he'd started noticing that his baseball buddy had a body built for sex as well as sports, he'd felt crazy, unsure— like a schoolboy again. He wasn't supposed to be sexually attracted to T-bone, yet he was having erotic dreams about her. How screwed up was that?

Maybe the doctors and his dad were right—his brain needed fixing as much as his body did.

Earlier tonight he'd been chasing bogeys, dreaming up a threat where none existed. He'd been so damn sure that someone had been hanging around for some dark, sinister purpose. Every cell in his body had gone on alert, just as it had on countless missions in danger-ridden battlefields. Turned out his "enemy" was probably just a kid who'd been forced to toss a snack he wasn't supposed to have.

He was getting rusty. Even if his body could cut it, he was losing the edge that had made him not just a member of the team, but the team's leader. The longer he stayed away from Special Ops, the more impossible it would be for him ever to return.

However, tonight, with Tess, those insecurities he didn't even want to acknowledge hadn't mattered. He hadn't just been the man Tess wanted. He'd been the man *he* wanted to be.

For an hour.

But as they'd cleaned up and dressed in the concession stand afterward, he'd had a moment to think beyond the four walls of that tiny building where he'd been Superman for a while.

What if that was a fluke? Could he prove himself again? As a Marine? As a man?

And had he traded half a lifetime of friendship for one hour of feeling good about himself again?

"Hey, there are your buddies again." Tess punched him in the arm to get his attention.

Pulling out of his gloomy thoughts, Travis spotted the two young Marines crossing the street to where he now stood with Tess as she unlocked her car. Each man carried a clear plastic cup holding a golden liquid that was surely beer in them. "They're not *my* buddies," he insisted.

"Please." She stood in the triangle between the car, the open door and his body. "I've lived next to your family for almost twenty years. I recognize when someone's deferring to a superior officer. They must think you're running this town." She reached up and smoothed her fingers across a frown line that hadn't eased. "This block of it, at least."

"Well, if I'm in charge, then you'd better get inside that car where it's safe. I'll follow you home in Dad's truck."

"They're no threat."

"Humor me, okay?"

"Hey, sir." The short, blond kid called out.

Instead of doing what he asked, Tess turned to greet them. A damp breeze coming off the water and indicating a change in the balmy weather blew a corkscrew strand of hair across her face. She tucked it behind her ear and smiled as if they were all old friends. "Hey, guys. Did you have fun?"

"Yes, ma'am." The taller one with the dark hair grinned. "We're just gettin' started, though. We've got a motel booked for a couple of nights."

"Good." While Travis considered their plans a practical solution to keep two men who'd been drinking off the road, Tess seemed to think it was part of her job to play hostess to every Tom, Dick and Corporal who came to town. "I hope you enjoy the festival. Are you here for the fishing, the carnival or the crafts?"

The young man traded an eye-rolling glance with his friend.

Tess laughed. Her golden-streaked waves bounced against her shoulders in a casual muss, looking as if a man had run his fingers through it. He had.

"It wouldn't be the chance to meet a girl at one of the street dances, would it?"

The kid stared into his beer and blushed. Then he looked up at Tess. Looked at her as though she might be one of those girls he'd like to meet.

An uncomfortable feeling bristled down Travis's spine. "Was there something you wanted, gentlemen?"

The bite in his voice was sharp enough for Tess to slide him a curious look, but the two recruits had drunk too much to notice. Was that what he'd sensed earlier? Some young pup lusting after Tess? Looking at her in a way she claimed few men in Ashton ever had? Or was that the territorial twist his brain put on things after getting his rocks off with her?

The short one raised his nearly empty cup in a toast. "We just wanted to thank you for the tip, sir. The Bounty gave us our first drink on the house once we flashed our military I.D. They were real friendly to us there. Invited us back tomorrow night."

Travis didn't tell them that The Bounty catered to any military clientele because that was the heart of their business. If these two wanted to think they were something special, he'd let them. "Glad it worked out. Now if you'll excuse us."

He took Tess by the elbow and tried to get her into the car, away from the tall kid's ogling stare.

But the young men weren't done and she wasn't cooperating.

The shorter one pulled himself up as close to attention as a tipsy man could get. "We just wanted you to know that we appreciate the hospitality—we just got back from deployment. I'm Corporal Jaynes and this is PFC Thibideux. If you ever need anything, you call us."

What would he need with a couple of red-nosed—?

"Captain McCormick appreciates your offer, I'm sure." Tess piped in with a kinder answer than what he'd had in mind. "I'm Tess. If I run into you at the festival tomorrow or Tuesday, be sure to say hi."

Thibideux beamed at the invitation. He hadn't taken his eyes off her the entire time. "Yes, ma'am. Tess, I mean. We will."

If Tess were manning a kissing booth instead of a concession stand tomorrow, Travis got the feeling that Thibideux would be the first in line. And the second. And the third. Morty Camden might have passed over Tess to ask out her sister, and dozens of eligible men in town might have overlooked her, but these two men— Thibideux, in particular—admired what they saw. She might be an older woman to them, but if she were available, they'd be hitting on her.

If she were available. That bristly feeling wouldn't go away. Maybe it was the hour and he was tired, or maybe he was still struggling with a few of those insecurities. Travis slid his hand to the small of Tess's back in a subtle but unmistakable gesture of propriety.

He might have made a deal that whatever happened between them would be over in two weeks, but for two weeks he had the right to be territorial. "Move along, boys."

"Yes, sir. Ma'am."

"Yes, sir."

Obeying the curt dismissal, the two men said good-bye and disappeared back into the night.

"Good thing you're not on the PR committee." Now, Tess got into her car.

"I helped set up the concession stand, didn't I? I'm doing my part for Ashton."

"Is something wrong?" Tess let him close the door, but she rolled down the window before he could leave for the truck. She tilted her head toward the stand behind them. Those hazel eyes were a little less sure of themselves than they'd been a moment ago. "Did I miss something? What we did in there was okay, wasn't it? That spontaneity is what an affair is all about, right?"

Was she talking *okay* in the sense that her performance had been mediocre, or the fact that they'd acted like a real couple instead of a pair of friends helping each other out?

The first possibility was easier to address. Travis leaned in through the window and planted a firm, don't-argue-with-me-woman kiss on her mouth. He lingered long enough to feel desire stirring through him again. Her sweet, succulent lips were bruised and swollen and asking for more when he pulled away.

"What happened between us can't be defined by any simple adjective." He was reluctant to straighten and pull away from the sultry essence of her that filled the car's interior. But he was the one with issues, not her. He had to make her understand. "You were amazing. In baseball terms you were a grand-slam home-run."

He twirled his finger into one of the kinks of caramel-colored hair that hung loose against her neck. "I remember in college one time—I don't remember the girl's name," he shrugged in embarrassment, "but I remember the kiss. I'd just broken up with my girlfriend, and I was looking for... I don't know. A connection. Validation that I still had it. The details are hazy, but I picked her up in this bar and... let's just say we shared the kiss that all other kisses in my life are measured by." He spoke the truth. "Tonight topped that one."

The corner of her mouth that had begun to curve up in a smile flattened instead. Suddenly, she was very busy checking her lights and fastening her seat belt. "Well. Your dad's out to sea all day tomorrow, isn't he? I guess I won't be seeing you until he gets back. Give me a call when he returns and I'll cover for you."

"Tess?"

"T-bone, Travis." She corrected him as if he'd called her Butch or Fred. "I'm still the same old T-bone. Don't worry. I've got your back."

Okay. Probably shouldn't have brought up another woman when trying to explain how great she was. Normally, he made better choices when talking to the opposite sex. Of course, what about his life had been normal lately?

"Tess," he insisted, holding onto the edge of the door, "I don't regret for one minute what happened between us. You said this was a fling we were having. I don't want tonight to be the end of it."

"Fine. It's not. It won't be." She started the car and shifted into gear, forcing him to release his grip and back off a step. "I have an early morning and a big day tomorrow. I need some sleep. You can follow me home if it'll make you feel better. But I promise, I've been driving home by myself for years. I'm perfectly safe here in Ashton."

There was no point in arguing any further—she was done listening and he'd run out of excuses. "You're safer with me on your tail. Goodnight."

"'Night."

He followed her practical, midsize sedan home in his dad's truck and sat in his own driveway until he saw the light go on in her bedroom window upstairs. Then Travis pulled into the garage and entered the deserted house.

He removed his T-shirt, kicked off his shoes and punched the blinking message light on the answering machine. He grabbed an ice-pack for his knee and a beer for his mood and paused to listen to his father's voice.

"Hey, son. Just checking in to make sure Tess isn't working you too hard. It's seventeen hundred hours and we're moving east toward Longbow Island. We'll be out of range soon, so I'll use the radio tomorrow to check in at about eleven hundred hours, before we head back."

Travis eyed the weather scanner on the counter beside the phone and remembered how the breeze off the bay had picked up before they'd left downtown. He briefly considered getting on the radio himself, but he'd wake them up if he called now. Whether they were anchored on the boat or set up in tents on the island, his father would be monitoring any storm fronts that could affect weather conditions.

Tipping his head back for a long, cold drink, Travis listened to his father continue on. "Eileen's the only one who caught anything today." Hmm. She'd gone from "that woman" to "Mrs. Ward" to "Eileen." "A twenty-five-pound striper off the stern. Beginner's luck."

"No such thing as luck, Dad. Just a good teacher." Like his dad.

Maybe one day he'd have the patience and the single-minded determination to teach something useful to someone. For now, he'd have to content himself with coaching Tess on her journey to uncover her sexuality. Apparently, he wasn't doing too bang-up a job of that. For a while there, they'd made magic together. If any other men had seen her with that come hither look in her eyes, they'd be lining up in droves to take her out.

But the confident gleam hadn't lasted. It was his own damn fault for not saying the right thing at the right time. "I'll do better tomorrow, T-bone," he promised, lifting his bottle in a blind salute. "I'll make sure you get what you need."

Travis tossed his shirt into the hamper and limped toward the guest bedroom. But at the bottom of the stairs, he changed his mind. He was restless enough as it was. Perhaps the familiarity of his own bed in his own room would help him relax.

Aching from fatigue more than any real stress, his knee throbbed by the time he'd reached his room. Without turning on a light, he stripped down to his briefs and lay on his bed near the window.

But sleep wouldn't come. And he was honest enough to admit that the quest for sleep hadn't really brought him up here, either.

The view into Tess's window was obscured from the street. But here in the bedroom where he'd lived for so many years, he could look straight across their yards into her room. Even with the curtains drawn across her window, he was fascinated by the shades of movement.

What was she doing in there? Coming out of a shower? Brushing her hair? Changing into pajamas?

Hell. After all these years, he didn't even know what she slept in. Probably a baseball jersey. That would show off the toned length of her legs. Or something flannel. Then she'd be soft and cuddly. Wait, this was July.

Maybe nothing at all.

Travis groaned and rolled over onto his back at the memories *that* image conjured.

Who'd have thought—the girl next door screaming as she came beneath his mouth like that? He closed his eyes and replayed every sweet, satisfying moment in his mind.

Minutes later he opened his eyes and turned to her window again. The curtains were dark now. She had to be exhausted after that escapade. He grinned with silly male pride at wearing her out—and was humbled by how exhausted, yet sated, she'd left him.

But the grin rapidly faded.

And humility quickly turned to regret. He'd been jealous tonight, jealous of that kid making goo-goo eyes at her. That's what she wanted, wasn't it? To radiate that sexy confidence that made a man sit up and take notice?

As if his life wasn't already complicated enough— how was he going to walk away from Tess at the end of two weeks with their friendship intact, the way he'd promised? Jealousy had no place in a friendship like theirs. Of course, for that matter, neither did lust.

Long ago, Travis had learned that a deep, emotional investment in a relationship only doomed it to failure. He'd been shredded inside when Stacy had dumped him. He'd been young and rash then—too stupid to know how to keep a girl happy. And there'd been another woman—Gail—who'd claimed to love him, but hadn't loved the danger of his job. He'd thought about settling down then. But, ultimately, the job had won out over her inability to give her fears and doubts a rest.

The Corps was a mistress who'd never failed him—until a year ago.

Between Gail and the accident, he'd contented himself by moving from fling to fling. He was a natural flirt. As long as both partners were satisfied, he could enjoy the sex, enjoy the fun and move on. And he'd never once been jealous.

Two weeks with Tess should be no different.

But it was.

Travis didn't fall asleep until the first rosy light of dawn bloomed across the bay.

9

"UH-HUH."

There must have been something telling in the way Tess and Amy dragged their feet down to breakfast the next morning. Maggie McCormick put away the china cups and got out two giant mugs to fill with coffee for her grown daughters.

"Sit." As she set plates with omelets and English muffins at the table, it became clear to Tess that her mother was bustling about with the intent of going out soon. But she suddenly stopped, propped her hands on her hips and looked back and forth at her two summer visitors. "Is this something that requires me calling Nancy and telling her she has to check out the craft and antique show without me?"

Tess looked across the table and thought that Amy's ponytail was just about as messy and haphazard as the one she'd made with her own harder to manage hair. Did the soft shadows of fatigue beneath her sister's eyes match her own as well? Apparently, they'd both had a tough time getting to sleep last night.

"No, Mom. You go on to the festival," Tess insisted, inhaling the reviving scent of the rich hazelnut coffee before taking a grateful sip. "I have to be at the hospital this morning myself so I can't dawdle. I'm just pooped. I stayed up too late with…Travis last night."

Her body tingled with memories of last night's powerful seduction. She'd even been a little hoarse when she'd first woken up this morning. But the discovery of such physical joy had been quickly tempered by the humiliating admission that he remembered that passionate collegiate encounter, after all. She just hadn't been impressive enough for him to remember that woman was *her*.

Maybe she deserved to be stuck in a small town where an influx of interesting, eligible men happened only once a year.

She'd offered Travis her body and her heart that night all those years ago, and she'd been rejected by a man who'd sobered up and moved on to the next woman without even considering that good ol' T-bone might be the girl of his dreams. Or at least, his bed.

She was pretty much the same woman now she'd been back then—a little older, a little wiser, a little more experienced, sure—but the feelings she had for Travis were startlingly similar. She wanted to be more than a sly way to give his body the physical workout he needed. She wanted to be more than an available outlet for his obviously frustrated sexual needs. She wanted to be more than a summer fling. Had she really been a grand-slam home run last night? Or had she just made a fool of herself over a man she shouldn't want all over again?

Hiding her face behind another long drink, Tess hoped the steaming brew would explain away the confusion heating her cheeks. Her mother would never suspect that she'd been up late trading orgasms. Tess and

Travis had often stayed out late sharing long conversations about love and life and baseball. But she wasn't up for twenty questions, and she certainly didn't want to lie about her complex feelings and obsessive desire for the man next door.

"How is Travis doing with his therapy?" Fortunately, Margaret didn't suspect anything less than innocent had kept Tess up so late. She carried her own empty plate to the sink and rinsed it for the dishwasher. "Just to look at him, he seems healthy as a horse. But have you noticed the extra lines beside his eyes and mouth? Part of it is that outdoor living he loves, but I thought he looked older than I expected at the party."

"I'm sure it's fatigue, Mom. He's had a lot to recover from this past year."

"Well, he isn't that same carefree young man who used to jump out of my rose bushes and startle me when I went outside to hang up laundry." Ah, yes. That had been a favorite pastime for what, three? four? years. Her mother was right—Tess had only seen glimpses of that boyish personality in Travis since his return. He'd become much more moody. More serious. Edgier. And if possible, that made her want to be an important part of his life all the more. "He has burdens on his shoulders that he never used to have. Could be the job. Your father came home from Vietnam with the same hard look to him. The experience changed him somehow. I had to learn to accept the new man he was, and fall in love with him all over again."

Tess's heart welled at the fond emotion she heard in her mother's voice. They all had an empty place in their hearts that her father's love used to fill. She stood and wrapped an arm around her mother's shoulders. "We were lucky to have him, Mom."

"That we were."

Amy rose and joined them on the opposite side. "He was a good man."

Maggie nodded and hugged them both before shooing them back to their seats to finish breakfast. "So is Travis McCormick. I didn't mean to imply otherwise. I just hope he works through whatever's troubling him. He's lucky he has a trusted friend like you he can talk to."

Tess choked down a bite of cheesy egg that suddenly tasted like rubber. Right. *Talk.* Except for that first night on the beach, she and Travis hadn't exactly done a lot of talking. He'd pointedly steered their conversations toward a new topic whenever anything serious had come up. Like returning to Special Ops in two weeks. Like following doctor's orders toward as full a physical recovery as possible. Like fear of failure or mistaking awakening desire for falling in love. None of those topics had been open for discussion, though she imagined he sorely needed to talk. Maybe she should concentrate more on being there for him as a friend and worry less about whether or not she made a lousy lover.

"And you?" Maggie refilled Amy's coffee, thankfully turning her concern to her other daughter. "What makes you so cheery this morning?"

"Phone call from Barry."

Enough said. Maggie Bartlett had no problem calling a spade a spade. "What did the Butthead want this time?"

"Sympathy. His girlfriend dumped him."

"Maybe that bimbette is smarter than we gave her credit for."

Finally, all three of them could share a laugh and Tess began to feel rejuvenated for the coming day. She still had issues to resolve, but support from her family would never be one of them.

With worries for her children temporarily appeased, Maggie snapped on her fanny pack and prepared to join her friend for some serious shopping. "The three of us are still on for lunch, right?"

"Absolutely."

"You bet, Mom. You'll have to show us all the treasures you and Nancy find."

Maggie tucked in a folding umbrella as well. "Be sure to take your umbrellas or rain-coats. We're supposed to have a storm coming in late this afternoon or this evening." She popped her hand over her mouth. "Oh, my goodness. You two are grown women. You both have sense enough to come in out of the rain. And if you don't, it's *your* problem. Right?"

They laughed again.

"Hugs all 'round? Love you." Maggie kissed Tess's cheek. Then she hugged and kissed Amy. "Love you. You know, Morty Camden is a very nice man. You could do worse, believe me. Wait, you have done worse. Still love you."

"Bye, Mom." Amy urged her toward the door.

"Bye."

Once they'd sent Maggie on her way to the festival, Tess sat down to quickly polish off the last of her breakfast. "Ooh. A 'nice' rating from Mom. Is that the kiss of death for a date with Morty?"

Amy rolled her eyes. "I already said yes. It was the least I could do after dumping on him after talking to Barry last night."

"I bet that wasn't pretty."

"Not very. But since Morty didn't run away, I figured I owed him. So he's taking me to dinner and then along the historic Bay Walk to see the old shops that are open late this week." Amy poured the last of her coffee down the sink and started loading the dishwasher. "I guess we'll see if I can be content with nice and boring, or if I'm destined to have another bad boy in my future." She winked over her shoulder with a suggestive smile. "Are you and Travis planning another late night?"

A wink? Was Amy still hoping for a permanent union of the Bartlett and McCormick clans? "Just what do you think is going on between Travis and me?"

"Something interesting, I hope. His nickname *is* Action Man."

Tess refused to be baited by Amy's nudge-nudge, wink-wink tone. Sex normally was a subject she was comfortable discussing with her sister, but until she had a better idea of where this was going with Travis—or if their two week deal would even continue after last night's embarrassing retreat—Tess wasn't prepared to share. She rinsed and added her dishes to Amy's stack. "I have to work the concession stand until the street dance is over."

"Maybe he'll pay you a surprise visit."

"Maybe." The doorbell rang, saving her from more of Amy's romantic speculation. "I'll get it."

Tess returned to the kitchen minutes later, her arms filled with a cut-glass vase, a dozen long-stemmed red roses and a mystery.

"Wow." Amy dried her hands and came to the table to sniff the fragrant display. "Nice. Somebody spent a fortune on you."

"They can't be for me." Tess held out the card. "There's no name. It isn't signed, either. But the delivery man verified it had been ordered for our address. I have no reason to expect anything like this. You?"

Amy raised her hands in surrender. "Don't look at me."

"What about Barry?"

First, a phone call, then an expensive gift to score some points. It wouldn't be the first time Amy's ex had tried to buy forgiveness. "He wouldn't dare."

"He wants you back."

"If he thinks this'll do the trick, then he knows damn well where he can stick his roses. Besides, he'd take credit for it if he'd spent this kind of money. What does the card say?" Amy's frown echoed Tess's own confusion as she read the typed message out loud. "'Can't wait to see you again. I'll find you when the time is right.' Huh?"

"Is it me, or is that message more creepy than romantic? 'When the time is right' for what?" Tess had a bad feeling about the extravagant gift.

Maybe the anonymous note was completely innocent. Poorly worded, but not a threat. But Travis had spooked her enough last night with his mysterious spy in the alley that the idea of a secret admirer for her or her sister held little appeal.

"Morty?" Tess suggested. She hoped.

"We haven't even gone out on our first date. Why would he send flowers?"

"To cheer you up?" Tess was exploring all their possibilities. "You were pretty upset last night."

"That'd be an awful lot of money to spend on a woman he barely knows."

"He likes you."

"I don't think so." Amy shook her head, expressing her doubt. "He doesn't strike me as the grand-gesture kind of guy." She snapped her fingers as an idea struck. "Maybe they're for Mom."

"That doesn't change the creep factor."

Amy agreed. "Wait a minute. Why wouldn't a man send flowers to you?" Her gaze wandered past the bouquet and landed on Tess. Big Sis thought she knew something. "These aren't exactly the type of flowers a man sends because you had a nice 'chat.' Is there something going on with you and Travis?"

"No," Tess answered automatically. Other than her father and a couple of prom dates, men had never sent her flowers. Of course, she'd never given a man a hand job behind the candy counter before, either. Maybe it was his way of thanking her? Apologizing? Encouraging her to try again? "Our relationship's not like that. It's..." completely skewed after last night's events.

"It's what?"

"It's none of your business." Taking in a deep, steadying breath, Tess slid the card into the pocket of her shorts, held up her watch and headed for the front door. Travis was the one she needed to be talking to about last night, not Amy. Even if she came off sounding like an insecure dope, he was the only one who could provide answers. "If I'm leaving early for lunch, I don't want to be late for work. I'll call the florist and see if they can track down the sender for us."

Amy followed Tess to the door. "I'll talk to Mom and

see if she knows anything. Things are getting that interesting with Travis, huh?"

Tess paused in the open doorway. She should have known her sister's curiosity wouldn't be easily dismissed. They had talked about so many things over the years in confidence and commiseration. But she wasn't sure she could explain what was happening between her and Travis—she wasn't sure she understood it completely herself. She wanted him, as a friend and as a lover, and maybe even as something more. She just wished she knew which role she should be playing.

"Interesting doesn't begin to describe it," she said and let the door bang shut behind her.

"I WISH IT WOULD just rain and get it over with," Nixa Newhaven fretted. "It's keeping away the tourists."

The ominous drumbeat of thunder rumbling in the distance drew Tess back to the service window at the front of the concession stand. Clouds were rolling in, high and wispy, bringing a tinge of green to the sky before the sun completely disappeared below the horizon. "Something's brewing out over the water, all right. Hopefully, it'll hit tonight and blow out this humidity that's been hanging on all day."

Weather had been the most exciting topic she'd discussed all evening. Not that Tess had had many customers to converse with. She'd even sent home the other volunteer with a visiting grandson because there just wasn't enough to keep two people busy. She held up the hotdog she'd wrapped in foil. "Ketchup, mustard, pickles or onions?"

"The works."

Tess returned to the work station and completed Nixa's order. When she slid the hotdog and drink across the counter, she couldn't help but recall how she'd sat on this very counter last night and let Travis have his way with her. She flattened her palms across the cool Formica and closed her eyes, replaying every gasp, every scream, inside her head. Remembering how she'd gripped the edge of the counter in glorious agony and—

"Tess?"

Tess snatched her hands away as if the venerable Miss Newhaven had actually caught her in the act. But it was a five-dollar bill the older woman held up, not an accusatory finger.

Breathe easy, girl, Tess coached herself. She wanted to change her reputation in Ashton, but she didn't want to be known as the village crackpot. Masking her startled panic behind an apologetic smile, she got Nixa her change, then grabbed the paper towels and disinfectant spray and cleaned the counter for the umpteenth time that day.

Another swipe still couldn't erase the erotic memory. And since Nixa didn't seem to be in any rush to leave her quiet dining alcove beneath the awning, Tess made another attempt at idle conversation.

"Business certainly has been slow tonight." Though not so slow that she could close up and go check out some of the waking nightlife herself. Every now and then a couple or group of friends would pass by, and most stopped for a snack or drink. "It's early in the week though, so I wouldn't worry. Crowds tend to start small and build up to Friday and Saturday, anyway.

Unless something dangerous blows in, I imagine the streets will fill up the way they have in the past."

"I hope so." Nixa nibbled through her hotdog with the ladylike reserve of a dowager empress, so Tess was a little taken aback when the older woman stuck her fingers in her mouth and noisily licked the smeared condiments from each tip. "Mmmm."

"Good stuff, huh?" Tess had to laugh.

"Divine." Nixa dabbed her lips with a paper napkin and giggled as though her gusto for fatty meat products was as naughty a secret as Tess's own favorite concession stand indulgence. "I look forward to one of these foot-longs every year. It's one of the few times I really blow the diet my doctor has had me on for ages."

"Sometimes, a gal's just got to live a little."

"I used to think that way." Nixa's euphoric smile was already beginning to fade. "I'm sure I'll be paying for this in the morning."

"But you enjoyed it, didn't you?" *Please let her say yes.* If Tess wound up the grande dame of Ashton, Virginia, forty or fifty years down the road, she didn't want to be so set in her tame, predictable ways that she couldn't even splurge on one hotdog.

Tess breathed a sigh of relief when Nixa nodded.

"I did. It's nice to know there are some traditions we can depend on year after year." Nixa reached through the serving window and patted Tess's hand. "Just like the town depends on you, dear."

How could a compliment sound so sad? Had Nixa ever yearned for something more than what she had? Were there adventures in her life to look back on? Affairs? Summer loves?

The wind suddenly picked up, whipping a cool, damp blast of air off the bay. Nixa made a grab, but her napkin and paper cup blew off the shelf. "Oh, my."

But before she could turn and scoot after her trash, a man appeared. He stomped the cup to anchor it while he bent down to collect the napkin. Then he straightened to a good six feet of well-proportioned height.

"Here you go, ma'am." The thirtyish man in pressed jeans and a silky cotton shirt gave the items a gallant toss into the trash.

Nixa smiled coyly, blushing at the attention. "Thank you."

"My pleasure."

Tess might be blushing, too, if the raven-haired hunk had turned that sexy, megawatt smile on her. He lacked the scars and laugh lines that gave Travis's face such interesting character, but dress those broad shoulders and chiseled features in a uniform and he could be the poster boy for whatever branch of the military he obviously served in. Yum-mee.

"Well…" Was Nixa preening? She smoothed her flawless silver hair from her forehead to her neck, and patted the trim bun at her nape. "Welcome to Ashton. It's so nice to meet a gentleman with manners."

"I find I catch more bees with honey than with vinegar, ma'am."

"Too true. Too true." The prim, predictable Miss Newhaven was flirting with the young stud! Tess didn't know whether to cheer the old girl on or bemoan the fact the guy hadn't even noticed her yet. After another few exchanges about the coming storm and festival events, Nixa turned to acknowledge her. Her normally wan cheeks had flushed a healthy pink. "Goodnight, dear. I'd better be going. I'm not fond of driving after dark."

"Goodnight, Miss Newhaven."

"Enjoy your evening, ma'am."

"Enjoy yours."

After Nixa's departure, Stud Man pulled out his wallet and walked up to the window. From this angle, she could see that the man's eyes were a clear icy blue—beautiful in color, but mysteriously hard to read. They sure grew 'em handsome wherever this guy came from.

"What can I get you?" Tess asked.

He looked through the screen to the displays inside. "What's good?"

"Everything. Depends on what you're hungry for." Maybe it was this guy who brought out the flirt in women of all ages. Suddenly, every innocent word they exchanged seemed laden with a double meaning.

"What do *you* recommend?"

"Depends on what you're in the mood for. Something spicy? Something sweet?"

"I like that combination."

Then again, maybe she was learning a trick or two about how she presented herself to men from her encounters with Travis. "Okay, then a hotdog or nachos? And how about something chocolate?"

"Hotdog. No pickles," he said and Tess slid around the display shelves to begin filling his order. "And I'll take the chocolate peanut butter cups and an iced tea."

"You're in town for the festival, I assume?"

"I've been here a few times over the years. Actually, I'm looking for an old friend. Maybe you know him. He's sort of a local hero type."

Tess wrapped the ends of the foil around the hotdog. "I might. What's his name?"

"Travis McCormick."

Travis. I want you. Holding the warm dog in her hands instantly took her back to last night again. She barely suppressed a crazy urge to giggle at the thought. Her hands trembled and every pore in her body suddenly sprang open to release the heat surging inside her. Man, she had to get away from this food, this shack, so she could quit thinking about sex with Travis. How badly she wanted it, how desperately she wanted to improve her skills so that, drunk or sober, he would know it was her each and every time they came together. She wanted to shake this driving need to know that, no matter what form it took, their lovemaking would be a memory worth keeping.

But with no escape from her present drudgery in sight, she quickly set the food on the counter and sought out a colder task to cool her libido. She took her time filling a cup with ice and adding cold liquid before trusting herself to speak calmly and coherently again. "I know Trav. I haven't seen him tonight, though. Did you two serve together?"

"Back in the day. Since I was in town, I thought I'd buy him a drink."

"Are you from Special Ops, too?"

"No, I'm with the promotions and personnel department. I make sure we have the right people where they need to be."

"Oh?" Oh. Maybe she'd been worrying about the wrong problem. Did this man bear the news Trav had been waiting for? More importantly, was it what Trav wanted to hear? Or would this man's announcement destroy the career and ego of her very best friend? "And you want to talk to Travis? Is it important? I could call him."

"You know him well enough to get him away from whatever he's doing?"

She wouldn't have offered, otherwise. "Yes."

For a few silent moments, he held her gaze and considered her offer. But then he shrugged off her curiosity. "Nah, it's not that big a deal. I just thought if he was around, I'd buy him a drink. I can call him myself if I need to."

Oh, no. This man wanted to meet Travis in person. That couldn't be good. Man-to-man, face-to-face—that's how these military types delivered bad news. Her father had been like that: call a man ASAP with good news, but wait until you could look him in the eye to deliver bad news.

"Well, if you give me your name, when I see him, I'll tell him you stopped by."

Officer Studmuffin bit off the end of his hotdog and chewed slowly, savoring his meal as much as Nixa had. Those ice-blue eyes held her gaze, giving Tess plenty of time to wonder and worry what this might be about. Her toes were dancing inside her tennis shoes by the time he swallowed. "You said *when*, not *if*," he pointed out. "So you expect him later?"

"I hope—"

"Tess!"

The blue ice blinked and looked away as PFC Thibideux and Corporal Jaynes waved to her from across the street. They hurried over, smiling and chatting.

"Remember us?"

"How could I forget?" She grinned at their boyish efforts to spruce themselves up before they reached the stand. Crew cuts and clean-shaven faces required very little maintenance. "Need a snack before the dance starts?"

"We thought we'd come and flirt with you first."

"Yeah, get our engines warmed up."

She laughed at their shameless efforts to charm. But the black-haired hunk seemed less impressed. Had he intentionally slid back in front of the service window just as Thibideux reached the counter? It wasn't very comforting to think that this man's purpose in Ashton was serious enough that he would brush another man aside to be first in line. "Tess. I always liked that name. It's as pretty as you are. Tell Travis I was looking for him."

"I will."

Travis's old friend wasn't all doom and gloom. One ice-blue eye closed in a suggestive wink. "You were right about the sweet and spicy. Very nice."

"Thanks."

As storm clouds crept across the moon and darkened the town in a breezy night, a dozen more customers wandered into line behind Jaynes and Thibideux. Suddenly Tess was busy—and the handsome flirt was gone before she realized he'd never given her his name.

"Yeah, Dad. Longbow Island. You'll be there a second night. Got it." Travis jotted the information onto the notepad beside the ham radio equipment in his father's study.

"The wind's…"

"What's that, Dad?"

The hum of static that made Hal McCormick sound

as if he were speaking from inside the bilge box on his boat popped like an electronic thunderclap. Probably another lightning strike in the atmosphere. Several seconds of silence followed.

"Dad?" An antsy feeling tickled the back of Travis's neck and crept down his spine. "McCormick base to Helena Two. Repeat. McCormick base to Helena Two. Dad? You there?"

A crackle of static answered.

"Dad?"

Travis shoved his chair back from the radio console. The wires didn't give him much leeway, but he needed room to pace. Answer me, Dad. He tapped at the earphone and muttered out loud. "Answer."

He'd been in the field often enough with dangerous weather, damaged equipment or no equipment at all and managed to survive. He'd been through years of training to avoid panic at the first sign of distress, to take stock of a situation, evaluate options, and then take action only if need be.

If the weather turned bad, he could deal.

If the radio malfunctioned, he could fix it.

If he had to ensure his own survival and the safety of a fellow Marine and two civilians, he'd improvise.

But Travis's years of experience hadn't prepared him for standing by while his sixty-year-old father, who took a pill every morning to keep his heart from going haywire, coped with the very same challenges.

When Hal had missed their agreed-upon check-in time, Travis had worried a little. His dad was probably at the stern, hauling in a marlin or a shark who wouldn't surrender. He'd still be home by sunset.

But when two hours had passed and he couldn't raise his father on the radio or the cell phone, then four hours, Travis had stopped pacing on his sore knee and called the harbor master. Squall lines over the Atlantic had hit earlier than predicted. The Helena II was one of several boats that had checked in with a change in arrival time. Hal planned to wait out the storm and sail in tomorrow. Everyone was fine. The boat was fine. No need to worry.

Hell. The whole idea of sending his dad on this excursion was to ease up on his stress. But if Hal was battling the elements, battling equipment—and likely battling Eileen Ward's fear of the water, which would only be intensified by the storm and rough seas—then his blood pressure must be going through the roof. What had Tess told him when he'd been so anxious to ease his father's concerns about him? *Families worry. That's what they do.*

He supposed this was a good taste of what his father had been going through over a son who'd been blown to bits and knitted back together. Damn. "C'mon, Dad. Answer!"

Man, he wished Tess was here. She'd always been a calming, sensible influence on him. She'd been there for breakups and losses. She'd been with him through letters and prayers and e-mails in the middle of perilous war zones and tedious base assignments. She knew when to listen, when to hug, when to scold.

He could use a friend like that right about now.

But she was working. And he'd been a jealous butthead—or at least something had shut her down after that amazing make out session last night. He needed to apologize before calling in another favor. Hell, they needed to talk so he could find out what was wrong and make it right.

In the meantime, Travis tried to recall the comfortable memory of talking to Tess underneath the pier afer his welcome-home reception. But all he could come up with was the heated memory of Tess's ass snugged against his crotch during a makeshift game of stickball, or the image of her screaming in ecstasy around the melting sweetness of a chocolate bar.

"Damn it." Travis punched his fist against his palm. It was getting to the point that he wanted to be with Tess—he wanted to be *in* Tess—just as much as he wanted to be reinstated to Special Ops. The line between friend and lover was blurring. At the end of two weeks, he knew he'd lose Tess in one role. But if he wasn't careful, he'd lose her twice.

And then there'd be no hugs, no scolding, no gentle smiles to get him through tense nights like this one.

Travis picked up the microphone and raised his voice as though volume alone could clear the airwaves. "Dad, come in."

A high-pitched sound screeched across his eardrums. "Ow! Damn." He ripped the headphones off and held the tortuous sound at arm's length until he could adjust the decibel level. His father was scrolling through the radio dial, finding a working frequency. He held the headphones to one ear and sat back down as static returned to the line. But there was still no voice. "C'mon, Dad. Make it work."

"…Two to McCormick base. Travis?…there?"

Hallelujah! "I've got you now, Dad. But you're breaking up."

"…fine, son. …Coast Guard apprised…ride it out with Eileen and…see you tomorrow."

His elation at hearing his father's voice was tempered by all the ways he could interpret that garbled message. "Dad? Verify situation okay."

"Verified." His father was shouting now, too. But his voice was strong. When it came through. "…call… storm over. See…tomorrow. Helena…out."

Travis pulled the headset from his ear and breathed a sigh of measured relief. "McCormick base out."

He shut down the power and tried to believe that his father did have everything under control. The man was an old sea salt, who could probably navigate the waters of Chesapeake Bay and the near Atlantic coast and islands with his eyes closed. He and Craddock were veteran Marines with survival training from back in the day. And he couldn't discount the feisty powerhouse Millie Craddock, either. The forced proximity might even give his dad and Eileen the opportunity to find some common ground so they could get along. They would be just fine.

It wasn't until he left the static and panic of the study and entered the quiet of the rest of the empty house that Travis realized the rain had started here, too. He went to the sliding glass doors and looked out over the deck and beach to the bay beyond. The gray water looked black tonight, with no moon or stars to reflect off the surface. Flashes of cloud-to-cloud lightning sparked overhead, giving brief glimpses of the wind and rain churning the bay into deep, choppy waves. Rain slapped the door. Travis spread his hand against the smooth glass and felt how the front blowing ahead of the storm had cooled the air outside.

Nope. His dad didn't want to be out in this. Not on the water where the effects of the storm would be more intensified. Probably not even in a tent on the rocky beach of Longbow Island. But Hal and his crew would be safer if they stayed put there.

Some hero. Sitting on the sidelines while a group of older folks faced real danger.

Travis didn't want to be here. He didn't want to be alone tonight to worry about stuff he couldn't take care of himself.

He still owed Tess that apology. They still needed that talk.

Time to take action.

Grabbing his jacket and keys, and leaving the knee-brace behind, he dashed out to the driveway and climbed into his dad's truck. Inside, he smoothed the water from his scalp, checked the time, and threw the truck into gear. He could use a soda and some popcorn right about now.

His mission tonight was to reconnect with Tess.

Whether as friend or lover, the choice would be hers.

10

WHAT IF SHE hauled off and did something completely irresponsible? Like close the awning of the concession stand and walk away? Heck. Why bother closing the awning? Tess hadn't had a single customer the past hour. The evening drizzle had evolved into a steady rain, and the wind and lightning overhead meant the storm was going to get worse before it blew on through Ashton.

The band at the courthouse had packed up. The street dancers had moved into the local bars and restaurants or gone home. The carnival rides were shut down and the tourists clamoring for hotdogs and popcorn were nonexistent.

She should have brought a book to read. Or a radio so she could listen to the Washington Nationals baseball game.

Tess was going nuts, hanging around the concession booth with nothing to do but remember that that was the spot where Travis had pinned her against the door. That was the brand of candy she'd gnawed through when he'd gone down on her. That was the stack of cups they'd knocked over in their hasty efforts to get dressed again after the fact.

Tess propped her elbows on the counter, rested her

chin in her palms and leaned forward to let the wet air mist through the screen and cool her face. She tried scanning the corners and alleys, looking for Travis's suspected spy, but rain and the limits of the streetlights revealed nothing but bricks and concrete and shadows. She wished Travis were here; they needed to talk. A conversation with him was guaranteed stimulation, whether they laughed, debated, or explored the merits of more serious topics.

Of course, in years to come, she might always associate the concession stand with Travis McCormick and their naughty rendezvous. If he was here, *talking* might not be the first activity to cross their minds.

"Damn." Tess batted the screen in frustration, flicking the collected drips onto the sidewalk. She straightened and circled the stand, searching for something else to clean, prep or put away before her shift was over at eleven.

She and Travis really did need to talk. She'd decided to confess that she was the college encounter he'd compared her to last night. He had more sexual experience—perhaps he could help her understand how she could be forgettable one time and irresistible the next. How she could pour her heart and body into caring for him, and he could…forget her.

She didn't want him to feel guilty. She didn't blame him for being drunk. But so much of her own sexual confidence—or lack thereof—had hinged on that embarrassing encounter that she just needed some answers. How much of last night was just seizing the moment and helping a friend get what she wanted?

"Sounds like a *Dr. Phil* show." She fisted up a wad

of paper towels and wiped down the minifridge, which was already spotless. "Insecure woman competes against herself for the affections of a sexy man. And loses." Man, could she use a sympathetic sounding board right about now. "That's messed up, girl."

"If I'd known you were out here by yourself in the middle of the night, I'd have come by sooner." Travis's rich, mischievous baritone through the screen startled her.

"McCormick!" Tess pressed a hand to her thumping heart and then to the heat blossoming on her cheeks, buying herself a few moments to gather her composure and pray he hadn't heard those last few thoughts she'd spoken out loud. Not exactly the way she wanted *that* conversation to start.

"Who're you talkin' to? The voices inside your head?"

"At least I'm in good company." When she finally turned around, she saw the dark spots on his tan jacket where the rain had soaked his broad shoulders. His hair looked like liquid bronze slicked against his scalp. And in the light from inside the stand she saw the rivulets of moisture streaking his clean-shaven cheeks as he pressed his nose into the screen. She laughed at the teasing expression on his face and crossed to the counter. "Didn't your mother ever talk to you about hats and umbrellas and staying out of the rain so you wouldn't catch cold?"

"Yeah, but I wasn't paying attention that day."

"Did you ever?"

His devilish smile disappeared as he straightened to a military posture, and suddenly she could see the careworn lines her mother had spoken about that morning. "Seriously, T-bone, this street is deserted. And this screen wouldn't stop anyone from breaking in if he wanted to get to you or that cash box." He looked up and down the street. "All these shops are closed. With the street blocked off, there's no traffic. With the rain, there are no vendors, no pedestrians. And I can barely make out the din from The Bounty from here, so I doubt anybody around the corner would hear you if you screamed."

"Even the way I do it?" He was so damn serious she couldn't resist the tease.

He opened his mouth to add another argument, but slowly closed it and shook his head. "Yeah, even the way you scream." He swiped the moisture from his face, taking some of the tension with it. "Where's your car parked?"

"Far enough away that a smart woman would ask a certain strapping Marine to walk her to the parking lot when she's done."

"So are you done?"

She glanced up at the sheets of rain pouring off the edge of the awning. Judging by the steady staccato drumming on the metal roof, it wasn't letting up anytime soon. And a walk to her car would give her the opportunity to talk to Travis. "I don't think it would hurt to close up early." She pointed to the awning anchors through the screen. "Do you mind?"

In under five minutes, she had the building locked down, her purse zipped inside her windbreaker, and a ball cap wedged on top of her head. She and Travis got soaked to the skin as they hurried to her car. They were actually too busy jumping puddles and ducking downspouts to get much talking done. So when Travis tried to close the car door behind her, with an offer to follow her home, she snatched at his soggy sleeve and asked him to join her.

Beads of rain clung to his golden lashes when he winked. "If you don't mind a puddle in your passenger seat." He closed the door behind her, dashed around to the passenger side and climbed in.

Tess already had the engine running and the heat turned on to help dry them out and keep the windows from fogging. "So, since it's not really your job to patrol the streets of Ashton, what brings you out on a night like this?"

"Oh, damn, I forgot." He reached inside his jacket pocket and pulled out a bedraggled daisy. "Peace offering?"

Tess giggled at the sad little flower with its broken stem and smushed bloom. She rescued it from his big fingers and good intentions. "How sweet." She touched the swath of delicate white petals to her nose and inhaled the fresh, light scent. It would require a fair amount of TLC to revive it to its original glory, but it was the thought that touched her. "I like this better than the roses that came this morning."

"What roses?"

"A dozen long-stemmed red ones."

Travis shifted, trying to get comfortable in the small space of the car. "Who were they from?"

"Not you, apparently."

"No. Is there a secret admirer I'm competing with? Maybe a not-so-secret one?"

"Are you kidding?" She couldn't get used to the idea of one man showering attention on her, much less two. "They're probably not even for me. The card didn't say, so more likely, they're Amy's. Or even Mom's. Whoever sent them didn't sign the card, either. It was just a weird, typed message."

"How weird?"

"Something like 'I enjoyed our time together, and I'll find you again when the time is right.' That is weird, right?"

Travis's expression gave her her answer. The steely concern that had shadowed his gaze when he'd lectured her on nighttime safety risks darkened his blue eyes again, reminding Tess of the creepy feeling the roses had given her that morning. She leaned forward to stretch her back and roll the kinks from her neck, imagining that she could roll that unsettled feeling off her back as well.

Time to change the subject. She nodded toward the precious daisy. "So—what's this for?"

"An apology." Travis shrugged, then reached down to shove his seat back and give his long legs room to stretch out. The suspicions that had filled the car slowly dissipated, and a different kind of tension took their place. "Last night was…unexpected. But I was completely turned on. It was good for me, and I don't mean just physically. I should have thanked you for that. Thanked you better than I did."

"Trav—"

"But those noncoms came on to you and I got my nose all out of joint and… You don't think one of them sent you the flowers, do you?"

"Did either of them strike you as the type who could afford long-stemmed roses in a crystal vase?"

He shook his head, answering her question or still

condemning his own actions, she couldn't tell. Maybe both. "You know, what happens *after* a couple gets close can be just as important as the act itself." He arched one brow. "Or so I've had women tell me."

She laughed and swatted his arm. "I don't want to hear how many women you've had this discussion with."

He covered his heart with his hand. "Hey, I'm tryin' here. Whatever I said or didn't say, or however I screwed up, I'm sorry. You were amazing. Period. We don't have that much time together to start with. I don't want it to be over after just one night." He reached across the console between them. His fingertips hovered close to her lips, but never touched her. "There's more I want to show you."

Tess shivered at the portent in his husky voice. At the instant frissons of anticipation he could set off with a word or a look, she cranked up the heater to pass them off as a chill from the rain. But she wasn't any good at that sort of game, and Travis wasn't buying it.

Still clutching the daisy in one hand, she reached up and laced her fingers with his. "I don't want us to be over with yet, either. Last night was pretty cool. Very cool," she amended. "Hell, it was fantastic. And I want to do it—or something like it—again. But—"

"Damn." He squeezed her hand. "You ruined it with the *but*."

"*But*," she turned in her seat and insisted he listen, "I have something I need to tell you, and I'm afraid you'll change your mind about me—about us—continuing our training sessions."

"Not a chance."

"You haven't heard what I'm going to say yet."

"Anything you don't know I can teach you. Or we'll learn it together."

"It's not that."

"Are you worried about transmitting something?"

She blushed at that one. "No."

"I'm not, either, but I promise we'll be completely protected. I made a stop before I came here."

He bought condoms? "That's sweet."

"Sweet again? That's not what I'm goin' for."

"It's presumptuous, then."

"You just said you wanted to do it again."

"But there was a *but*."

"Son of a bitch, there was." Travis pulled his hand away and retreated to a polite distance. "Is this the kind of conversation we need to do over a cup of coffee or glass of beer?"

"Just listen. Please."

"Shoot, T-bone."

She took a deep breath and prepared to bare her soul. "That kiss? That make-out session in college—"

"Make-out session?"

"—the one you measure all other kisses by in your life?"

"What about it?" His breathing stilled and his hands came to rest on the faded denim covering his muscular thighs.

"Do you ever wish you could meet her again?"

"I thought you didn't want to know about the other women in my life."

"That was me, Trav."

"What was?"

"I was the girl who tracked you down at the third

bar you'd been to that night. It was me who took you home and let you crash on my couch. After Stacy left you for what's-his-face, I thought you needed a friendly face to talk to."

He waved aside the idea. "I wasn't interested in talking that night. I wanted to get laid. I was looking for someone who was into me, who made me feel like I still had the juice."

"I know. I made a bed for you on that hideous, orange-striped couch that came with the furnished apartment."

He paused. "I remember orange stripes."

Would he remember anything else? "I loosened your clothes and tried to cover you with a blanket so you could sleep."

"I thought she was seducing me." He pointed an accusing finger. "I've told you this story, haven't I."

"Never. You took my shirt off. Said you needed me, wanted to be in me."

Travis's eyes widened. "I wanted to bury myself inside that woman and forget all about Stacy."

She remembered the details vividly. His hands on her breasts. His kisses. The weight of his body on hers. Everything Tess had ever felt for Travis had altered and intensified that night. "The blanket kept getting twisted between us so—"

"—I balled it up and used it for a pillow."

"You kissed me. You said all great sex started with a kiss."

"Shit." He dipped his forehead into his hand, then scrubbed his fingers through his short hair, flipping water droplets onto the window and leaving bronze spikes in his wake. His eyes were unreadable when he looked at her again. "That was you? All these years and you never told me that we—"

"We didn't."

"We could have been…?"

"We weren't." They hadn't been lovers then, and unless she could salvage her pride, they wouldn't be lovers now. "I *was* trying to seduce you that night."

"You were succeeding."

"I didn't know what I was doing then any more than I know now."

"Dammit, Tess, I was drunk. I passed out. I wanted you like crazy."

"You didn't even know it was me that next morning. You wouldn't even consider that it *might* have been me you wanted to take to bed. You sat there drinking your coffee and going on about this babe you'd nearly screwed the night before. You asked me to help you find her."

"Ouch."

"I tried to tell you it was me." Temper flowed through her veins, along with shame and twelve years of thwarted desire. The daisy bit the dust as she shook her fists across the seat. "No way in hell could that sex goddess have been me. And now I'm supposed to believe that I'm *irresistible?*"

He caught her hands and pulled her toward him as he met her halfway. "Seduce me again."

The bold challenge shocked her into silence.

He gentled his grip, folding her hands between his. "I saw you last night. I heard you. I tasted you. I guarantee you, I'll never forget what you do to me."

Tess was shivering again, likely the adrenaline working its way through her system. She squirmed in her seat, watching the rain streak down the window beyond his shoulder. Finally, she found courage to look him in the eye. "Is that a dare?"

"Does it need to be?"

Her puff of laughter almost dissolved into a sob. She caught her bottom lip between her teeth and smiled through it. "I'm talking about a gap in self-confidence here."

"And I'm saying there's no reason for it."

He pulled his keys from his pocket, slid one off the ring and pressed it into the palm of her hand. A house key.

"Dad will be gone all night, and I'll be in that big house by myself. Alone. Waiting. I'm stone cold sober, too, if that means anything to you." He curled her fingers around the key and leaned over the console. His moist breath warmed her ear with a whispered caress. "Seduce me tonight. I guarantee it will be memorable. For both of us."

"I can't. What if I suck at it?"

He pulled away and opened the car door. His face creased with a classic Travis McCormick smile. "I know you won't."

She grabbed his arm to stop him from leaving. "How? How do I know you're not just saying that to spare the feelings of an old friend?"

Rain blew into the car and splashed her face. His jacket and jeans were getting soaked. Travis moved closer to drier territory, stopping just short of touching her lips with his. "Because you're good ol' reliable Tess Bartlett. And you haven't let me down yet."

Then his mouth closed over hers. His kiss was a reward, an apology, a demand. But it was done and he was gone before she could decide which message she should respond to.

TRAVIS WAITED AT his bedroom window, his sodden jeans dripping on the carpet, watching for the light to go on in Tess's room.

Just to know she was okay, he rationalized.

Because he'd been an ass twelve years ago and hadn't been able to connect "Tess" and "sex goddess" in his hungover brain, she couldn't quite believe that his attraction to her now was the real thing. Hell. *He* couldn't believe how badly he wanted her to take him up on his challenge.

She didn't need lessons from him on how to get a man's attention and drive him crazy. She didn't need lessons from any man. Tess just needed a chance to strut her stuff. She needed a man to see her for the delectable treasure she was.

And he wasn't about to let anybody else volunteer for that mission.

He'd seen her safely home. Half hoped she'd walk straight to his front door instead of up the steps to her mother's house. But she'd unlocked the door and disappeared inside her dark, sleeping childhood home without even a wave goodbye. Travis had been left standing in the rain, with the wind pasting his wet clothes to his skin.

He thought of his dad—said a prayer that he was dry, his stomach was full, and that he'd remembered to take enough of his pills for the morning. He thought of Clarksie and his S.O. 6 unit—how they'd be wrapping up their assignment and prepping for the flight home in less than two weeks.

He thought of a twenty-one-year-old woman who'd rescued him from himself and nearly taken him to heaven—and her thirty-three-year-old counterpart, an unwitting siren who rescued him from his own driving needs and haunting fears, and had the power to take him well beyond heaven.

There.

The light went on in the second floor window, creating a beacon of creamy white curtains that called to him through the rain-shrouded night. The sense of relief that washed over him, knowing Tess was safe, was quickly replaced by a spark of anticipation that caught inside him, gradually speeding his pulse. He could see an indistinct silhouette moving on the other side of that curtain. Was Tess undressing? Bundling up in something warm? Pacing off the length of her room and calling him every well-earned name in the book?

Travis toed off his squishy deck shoes and kicked them into the bathroom where he'd shed his wet jacket. His socks joined the pile before he returned to the window to keep vigil until the light in Tess's room went dark. It was a most fitting sort of punishment for a man who'd caused her doubt about her sexual talents, he supposed. To want a thing so much and be denied it was painful. He knew. Because he wanted the woman behind the curtain, but he was quickly learning that the real thing—the real woman—was far more addictive to his body, far more necessary to his sense of well-being than any fantasy.

He had her halfway naked inside his head when the phone rang.

An instant alertness snuffed out the lust coursing

through him. It could be news of his father. Maybe he'd found a clearer means to make contact. Travis read the number displayed and smiled. The burst of adrenaline quickly receded and a familiar heat licked through his veins, reigniting his desire.

Tess.

He punched the talk button. "Hey."

"I forgot to say goodnight." Her quiet voice sounded as if she were in the darkened room with him.

"Goodnight, T-bone."

She cleared her throat. The silhouette behind the curtain moved. "Could you call me Tess tonight? Or honey or darlin' or whatever?"

"Okay, Whatever," he teased.

"Travis."

I want you. He heard the seductive subtext in that one-word reprimand, and his breath caught in his chest.

He forced himself to exhale, then breathe in again, evenly, slowly. To control the rapid thumping of his heart.

She was doing it.

She was seducing him.

The Action Man tried to play it cool, but Travis Harold McCormick of the USMC had never wanted a thing as badly as he wanted this. Not even S.O. 6. But he had to put his own needs on simmer and let this night be about Tess and what she needed. He swallowed past the lump of desire in his throat.

"Tess." He gave her name as dark and sensuous a spin as he could. I want you. He encouraged her to continue. "You've got the ball."

"Three different men flirted with me tonight."

Ouch. Strike one to the old ego. Other men should

not enter the conversation when he was this primed for a woman. "Really? Am I supposed to be okay with that?"

"You should be proud of your star pupil."

He looked through the rain and the night and saw her silhouette framed behind the curtain at her window. "I am. But you're *my* pupil."

"One of them said he was looking for you. He's a friend of yours from the Corps. I forgot to tell you that earlier."

"What's his name?"

"I got busy and didn't get a chance to find out."

"I'm not interested in him right now, anyway." From his lookout point, he could make out that her position mirrored his own. The fence and houses and rain-soaked night shrouded her window to the world while offering him a private view of her room. Open the curtains, he silently urged. "Is that all you wanted to tell me?"

"Thank you for listening to me tonight. I've always been embarrassed that I wasn't special enough to notice."

"Don't believe it." Her silhouette moved. His hungry gaze darted to the glimpse of her fingers slipping between the curtains, like a batter spotting the pitch and taking aim.

"You know we've never been able to resist each other's dares."

"Open the curtains, Tess."

He held his breath, licked his parched lips, then damn near got a hard-on the instant the curtains opened and he saw her standing there. She'd moved a lamp close to the window, spotlighting her and leaving her room in darkness behind her. The ball cap was gone. Her damp hair hung loose about her shoulders, kinking into curls and clinging to her cheeks. The jersey she wore was soaked, too, and fit her trim curves like a second skin. Her lips moved against her phone.

"Travis."

"Tess."

He pulled his bed stand closer to the window and turned on the lamp so she could see him just as clearly. Just like when they were kids. Only there was nothing innocent about the signals they traded tonight.

"It's hot," she murmured, her voice a seductive pitch that stroked against his groin.

Too damn hot despite the chill of wet clothes sticking to his skin. Travis reached for the hem of his T-shirt. He peeled it off over his head and tossed it aside. Cool air hit damp skin, but his temperature seemed to keep rising.

He put the phone back to his ear. "It's hot here, too."

He thought he detected a slight nod. Then she set her phone on the corner of her bed and came back to the window to slowly, deliberately, unhook the buttons of her jersey, one by one. Travis watched in rapt fascination. When she reached the last button, well below her waist, his dick jerked as if she'd touched him there.

His own chest heaved in a stuttered breath as she slid the jersey off her shoulders. Her breasts thrust toward him, nearly touching the glass. He reached out and splayed his fingers against the cool, hard pane of his own window.

At first he thought it was a sudden chill, or maybe second thoughts, when she hugged her arms around her waist, hiding that smooth expanse of skin. "Tess, don't stop."

But she didn't have her phone, and she wasn't.

"Damn, woman."

She pulled her arms up beneath her breasts, lifting them, squeezing them together. Her plain white bra gleamed against her skin, highlighting each swell and curve, and if he used his imagination, each straining nipple.

Leaning forward, she pressed her breasts against the glass and Travis's fingertips dug into the window with frustrated need. She dragged them in circles, finger-painting with each tit. His pelvis tilted in response.

When he'd dared her to seduce him, he'd thought it would be in person. But this was as innovative and compelling a turn-on as anything he'd experienced before. And his body was heating and tingling and rising to attention as if she were doing those things to him and not the glass.

"Tess." He whispered into the phone, knowing she couldn't hear. "Tess."

But she sensed his message, or felt the same electric current linking them across the night that he did. She retrieved her phone, and when she came back to the window, the bra was gone.

"How am I doing?" The soft question sparked an answer deep inside him.

"You're beautiful." She pressed her dusky nipples against the window. When she gasped into the phone, he felt the shock of hot skin meeting cold glass right along with her. "Touch yourself."

This was better than any fantasy his feverish dreams could conjure.

She slipped her free hand between herself and the glass, sliding the nipple into the crook of two fingers, squeezing, rolling, lifting, plucking. "Like this?"

Travis licked his lips, imagining his tongue there. Imagining the silky texture of her skin against his lips, the citrusy smell of her essence filling his nose. "Yeah." He heard the hoarse rasp that was his own need, begging for fulfillment.

She'd seen his tongue. She lifted her fingers to her own mouth and licked them, sucked them, moistened them with the same thoroughness as she had used when she'd sucked his cock last night.

"Yeah." He could barely make a sound. His knees were trembling, his hips were clenching, and he was rubbing himself against the window sill. He breathed in a moment of sanity and stepped back from the window. "You're killing me over here."

The witch smiled against the phone. "That's good, right?"

He couldn't answer. She twirled her wet fingers around her nipple. He heard her gasp again, saw her stomach jerk as she gave herself pleasure. She was panting hard—in rhythm with his own shallow breaths—by the time she'd unzipped her shorts and dropped them to the floor.

Tess was an erotic goddess, touching here, wetting her fingers and touching there. Travis unsnapped his jeans and was gently loosening himself from behind his zipper when she reached inside her panties and touched herself. Her eyes closed, her lips parted, her throat hummed an incoherent song of rapture.

He wrapped his hand around himself and squeezed, battling the urge to come before she'd completed herself.

"I'm hanging up now." She could barely get the words out.

"No!" But a click had disconnected them before he could get out his protest.

His shout rattled the glass. She disappeared into the darkness of her room. She would not do this to him. She would not leave him hanging. If this was some sort of tease, some sort of payback...

He tossed the phone onto his bed and sat down to peel off his wet jeans, his eyes still glued disbelievingly to the glass. He was as naked as she was when she came back into view.

Not a tease at all.

Travis braced his hands against the window, leaned his forehead against the cooling glass and gasped at the vision he saw.

How could he not have known? How could he never have imagined how perfectly sexy Tess was? How perfect she was for him?

How could he have had these feelings bottled up inside him for so long and not have known that he loved her? He wanted her? And he was the luckiest man on earth that she wanted him.

Tess had some sort of toy in her hand, a vibrator by his guess. She held the pad in her palm and pressed it between her legs. She spread them farther apart and moved her hand against her clit.

Travis's whole body lurched in response. Her mouth opened, her head tipped back, her breasts bobbed with each panting breath. She cried out.

"Tess," he whispered.

She clamped her lips shut, her hand still moving between her legs.

"Tess," he cried out with her.

Her breaths were coming faster and faster.

She froze for an instant. In ecstasy.

"Tess!"

Travis snatched the phone from his bed, the condoms from his jeans, and speed-dialed her number as he headed for the stairs.

Her breathless voice answered on the third ring. "Travis?"

"Get over here. Now."

_11_

TESS'S BODY WAS still weak from the aftershocks of her orgasm, made all the more powerful by Travis's greedy voyeurism.

Seduce me, said the man. If she wasn't mistaken, that desperate phone call meant she'd succeeded beyond her wildest dreams.

Well, maybe not her wildest. Not yet. As scarily fabulous as that naughty nighttime show had been, she still felt incomplete. So the seconds ticked by like eons as she stumbled around in the shadows to retrieve his house key from her purse, pull her trench coat from the closet and dash down the stairs without waking Amy or her mother.

Rain slapped against her overheated skin when she threw open the back door. She tied the coat around her naked body and ran barefoot across the yards and up onto Travis's back deck.

She needn't have wasted time searching for the key. Travis was there, opening the kitchen door. Closing it. Ripping at the belt of her coat and spreading it open.

"Tess." He ground the raw plea through tightly clenched teeth. She saw the condom already sheathed around his fully engorged member.

And then he had her off her feet. Up against the wall. And he was inside her.

"Oh-h-h." Tess moaned at the decadent pleasure of his long shaft squeezing inside her, stretching her, filling her. She wrapped her arms around his neck, her legs around his hips, opening herself, anchoring herself as he plunged into her once. Twice. Again.

"Tess." His strong fingers clutched her thighs. "Babe." His wicked tongue was in her mouth, mimicking every movement of his cock inside her. "I need you."

Her breasts pillowed against the hard wall of his chest. Her rain-slick skin shifted and rubbed against him, turning her nipples into sensitized pleasure points. "Travis."

"I need you." He ground his hips into hers, buried his face in her neck and cried out his release as she screamed his name and shattered around his last pulsing thrusts.

Moments later—minutes later?—she became aware that cool rain had turned to sticky sweat between their bodies. She savored the synchronous rhythm of their breathing slowing and deepening. She sensed that the man still holding her in his arms was spent.

Taking pity on him, Tess unwound her legs and slid her feet to the floor. Travis's penis slipped out of her slick center, but she wouldn't let him release her entirely. Instead, she wound her fingers behind his neck and thanked him with a teasingly tame kiss. "Ha!" she taunted, feeling more like a beautiful woman than she ever had in her entire life. "I dare you to forget me this time."

Travis rested his forehead against hers, looking deep into her eyes, understanding she meant no threat by her triumphant claim. Then they were laughing. Kissing each other gently. Wrapping each other in a grateful hug.

"That's one dare I'll walk away from."

Travis swung her up into his arms and carried her to the living room, taking her to a bed somewhere. She hoped. All of her baseball coaches had said that practice would improve her form. She intended to practice this new sport with Travis just as often as he'd let her. For as long as their time together allowed. But she could tell the instant his knee protested and quickly squiggled out of his grasp onto her feet.

"Damn." Tension crept in to destroy the relaxed satisfaction on his face. "Damn. Damn."

"Shh." Tess pressed a finger to his lips, silencing his self-critical curse. She spotted the sofa behind him and guided him to it. "You probably just overtaxed the joint. Let me take a look."

She spread out the afghan hanging over the back of the sofa. But when she nudged his chest, he refused to sit. He captured her hands and pushed her back to arm's length. But he held on, rubbing his thumbs across the back of her knuckles, searching for something inside himself before he raised his gaze from their hands to her eyes. "This isn't how I want you looking at me. I'm a man, not a patient. I don't want you to see me as some beat-up invalid."

Tess tilted her head, saddened by the pain that tightened his handsome mouth. She tried humor first. "Well, I don't know where you were, but the man in the kitchen with me was fully loaded." The double entendre barely earned the arch of one eyebrow. "I don't lust after my patients. I wouldn't do anything so daring—"

"—so beautiful," he added, releasing her to brush a curl off her forehead.

She buttoned the front of her coat, feeling more exposed by the emotions she was sharing than by his hungry eyes on her body. "I want to look at your knee because I care about you. It hurts me inside to see you in pain. If I can help, I want to. It's what I do, Travis. I help people feel better about themselves. But you're the first one who ever helped me feel better about me."

She let her gaze travel the length of his body, and made sure he understood she was scanning every well-defined inch of him. He was a magnificent brute to look at in his naked form—tall, strong, sleek. To her way of thinking, the scars webbing through the golden hair on his left leg and marking other parts of his body from jaw to toe only added realism, humanity and touchability to his perfection. She stopped when she reached the rich blue cobalt of his eyes. "When I look at you, I don't see a wounded soldier. I see a friend. I see a man who's honest with me, who makes me laugh. I see a man who listens to me when I get uptight about stuff and helps me get over myself."

Ah, at last, a smile. But he quickly shook it off and sat, his legs veeing out in a natural masculine position that only emphasized other intriguing parts of his form. "But I'm supposed to be this damned all-American hero, a man who almost died for his country."

She sat beside him. "You *are* a hero."

"For what? Thirty minutes at a time? Maybe two or three hours on a good day?" He squeezed his hand around his injured knee. "It's not just my body that's given out, T-bone. I used to be able to read the people around me, know who I could trust and who I couldn't. I used to be able to sense when the enemy was near."

He tugged the end of the afghan over his exposed lap, finally succumbing to a wane in self-assurance. "It's like I know it in my head—I know the skills, I have the experience—but I can't make my body do it when I need to. Not anymore. Not reliably." He plucked at the holes in the afghan. Tess reached out and laced their fingers together to offer calm and comfort. "A glitch in my response time, a misread instinct, a stumble—all could get me killed on a mission. It could get someone else killed." He tightened his grip around hers, seeking more than comfort. "Hell, since the accident, *I'm* the glitch. And it could keep me out of the Corps."

"That's not true, Travis." He looked as though he was about to argue with her, but she didn't give him a chance. "You told me yourself that there were hundreds of other jobs for Marines—and that every one of them was necessary for the Corps to run smoothly."

"I don't want to push papers."

"Then do something else." She climbed up on her knees beside him on the sofa and held her arms out wide to either side. "Reinvent yourself. Like I did. Like I'm doing. I'm a pro at dependability, consistency, providing support." She flipped up the collar of her trenchcoat, reminding them of what they had done together. "Who knew I could be such a shameless hussy?"

He started to grin. She almost had him. She punched his shoulder in a playful gibe. "And I was good at it, too, wasn't I?"

"You're proud of yourself, aren't you?" He palmed the back of her neck and pulled her in for a kiss. By the time they came up for air, the lines beside his eyes curled upward with laughter. "I will never think of you as a shortstop again."

Tess blushed at the fitting compliment only the two of them could share. As her body heated with renewed interest in the man beside her, she wondered how far down a blush could go.

Apparently, Travis wondered the same thing, too, because he pulled her into his lap and leisurely unfastened the buttons on her coat, letting the silky lining slide across her skin as the material parted, inch by tantalizing inch.

"So what can I do besides sneak behind enemy lines and find the bad guys?" he asked, forcing her to think when his hands and eyes made her want to feel. "What skills do I have besides shooting a rifle and blowing things up?"

"Well…" She gasped as the tip of one blunt finger brushed across the curve of her breast. "You're a pretty good coach. You know when to be patient, and you know when to push." He pushed his palm against that same breast and she moaned. Tess had to snatch his wrist and pull him away so she could finish her thought. "Maybe you could take your skills and experience and teach them to new recruits. They have teachers in the Marines, don't they?"

"Doesn't sound like a lot of action to me."

Um, was something stirring beneath her bottom? She braced her hands on his shoulders and tried to keep some distance so she could talk. "From everything I hear, having a roomful of students can give you more action than you'd ever want."

Travis lifted her, turned her, and sat her squarely in his lap so that there was no doubt about his growing erection or his intent. "I'll think about it," he promised, sliding the coat off her shoulders. "But I've never wanted anything else the way I wanted that job. Not until you, that is."

He kissed her tenderly, a marked contrast to the aggressive path his thumbs were taking along the inside of each thigh. "The action…" He touched her aching nub. "…not just…" Oh, Lord, she was losing it again. She palmed the back of his head and pulled him closer to deepen the kiss. "…job only," she finished disjointedly.

Travis lifted her up to take her breast in his mouth. Tess moaned. When he strode to the kitchen to fetch a condom, she gathered her thoughts into one coherent sentence. "Maybe you could find the action you crave elsewhere."

When he pushed her down onto the couch and settled between her legs, she had a good idea of exactly what type of action he had in mind.

And as he reduced her to babbling in a much gentler but no less meaningful joining than what they'd shared in the kitchen, Tess wondered how she was ever going to live without this funny, noble, caring man. And she wondered how her heart could survive going back to being just friends when their two weeks were up.

TRAVIS MCCORMICK was one lucky son of a bitch, thought Kyle Black. Even cut up into half a hero, the Action Man could get a woman to go to bed with him.

The rain pouring over his shoulders and plastering his dark hair to his scalp did little to cool the familiar temper raging inside him. He stood outside in the night, across the street, hidden in the darkness, seeing more than he wanted of McCormick's love life through the narrow window beside the front door.

But Kyle had seen enough. He couldn't resist sending those flowers, but that had been just playing around. Now he really knew what he had to do to make things right. He'd seen touchy-feely talking involved with this lay. McCormick cared about her.

Perfect.

Having General Craddock's return delayed by a storm out in the Atlantic would work to his advantage. It gave him the perfect excuse to make his presence in Ashton known—no more sneaking down after work hours and hiding in the shadows. What a loyal, dutiful soldier he'd be, driving down to check on his C.O.'s welfare. He'd be on hand to assist with any kind of rescue—he could offer the full resources of the DOD, if need be. With a practiced look of concern, he could be right there on the dock to welcome the Craddocks back to dry land.

And oh, yeah, maybe he'd bump into an old friend while he was in town.

Or an old friend's woman.

Kyle climbed inside his low-slung Firebird and used the hand towel beside him to wipe down the moisture that had blown in on his seat and door panel. After he'd toweled off his face and hair as well, he looked out at his surroundings and remembered. He'd come here dozens of times before without ever being detected. But in the past, he'd always come to watch the house next door. *She* was in there now. The woman he'd loved. The woman McCormick had taken from him just to prove that he was the better man.

Kyle wasn't sure what he felt for Amy Bartlett anymore. Wasn't sure he even cared that she'd run from his bed. But his feelings about McCormick were clear.

Time to make the bastard pay for all he had done.

And Tess Bartlett was the going price.

TRAVIS POPPED A gingersnap into his mouth from the tray of veggies, fruit and other snacks Tess had put together to replenish their energy after their late-night rendez-vous. He listened to the water running in the first-floor guest shower and had no problem picturing her strong, dexterous hands scrubbing soap across his favorite parts of her anatomy. Maybe even soaping up a few spots he hadn't discovered. Yet.

He grinned at the inevitable stirrings in his body and reached for his laptop to find a much-needed distraction. As much as he wanted to strip off his dry jeans and join her, he suspected both their bodies needed a chance to rest.

Tonight's training session had been intense. Against the wall in the kitchen, when he'd been like a madman and couldn't get inside her fast enough. That tender coupling on the couch. And then another after that when she'd been sitting on his lap and a debate about whether or not the Red Sox could ever again be World Series champions had gotten out of hand.

Sure, he had a year of celibacy to make up for. And she'd released her inner hussy in a major way. He was sure Nixa Newhaven and the old fogeys in Ashton who'd categorized Tess as the properly predictable Miss McCormick would be shocked at her wild lovemaking. And the blind men who'd overlooked her and made her think she was plain and forgettable could damn well eat their hearts out when they saw her with her hair down and her eyes lit with mischief.

Tess Bartlett was his.

When he returned to active duty with his unit, then those other men could buy her flowers and flirt and fall all over themselves to get her attention.

Other men. Travis jammed the power cord into the wall socket with more force than was necessary. He liked that scenario about as much as being told he could never be a Marine again.

She'd probably write him a letter or send him an e-mail to keep him posted on her progress. Just like those chatty notes with the hometown gossip that had entertained him over the years, except now *she'd* be the center of those stories—who had noticed her, who was hitting on her, who was taking her out.

Right. A note like that would drive him nuts. She'd granted him two weeks of seductive basic training. But now, instead of knowing he'd walk away feeling good about how two longtime friends had helped each other achieve their personal goals and mutual pleasure, he was feeling a little queasy about the whole idea of another man enjoying the fruits of her journey toward self-discovery.

He hadn't considered that feelings of possessiveness might come into play when he'd agreed to pursue this attraction—an attraction that must have been there all along, simmering beneath the surface—unnoticed, unexplored. Over the years, they'd needed each other as friends more than either had needed a lover. Or maybe those were just the roles they'd gotten used to playing. Tess had talked about how Ashton's residents were too set in their ways to see her as anything but a sexless tomboy and future spinster. Travis had been equally guilty of stereotyping.

It had taken a near-death incident to strip away his

cocky self-image. Ashton's Action Man could no longer guarantee his ability to charm a woman in every port, and the desire to do so had lost its appeal. With injury and uncertainty came a vulnerability he'd never experienced before, and with vulnerability came the need to trust on a level he'd never reached with any other woman. Who better to look to than an old friend for that kind of connection?

Maybe it was that unfamiliar need inside him that had finally allowed him to see Tess in a new way.

Nope, handing her over to another man at the end of this affair wasn't going down very well at all.

Smiling at the tuneless melody coming from the shower, Travis opened his laptop and typed a military address into a new e-mail.

Clarksie—

How's it hangin', Big Guy? Man, I still can't get over that one. No wonder Becky's so devoted to you. Can't be the good looks, eh? Seriously, man, you know she's counting the days until S.O. 6 is back in Virginia. Maybe even the hours. Minutes? Seconds? I know you are, too. As ready as we've always been to get ourselves into the thick of things, we were always more ready to head back home.

Travis looked up from the message he was typing and glanced over the familiar sights of his father's home around him. He'd made no secret of how little he'd wanted to return to Ashton this time. Coming home felt like quitting, like tossing in the towel and saying he was done with the Corps. But he'd done it—just to put his father's worries to rest and to show his superiors that he could still take an order, even one he hated.

But he'd never intended to stay. He'd never intended even to want to stay.

Was that driving need to return to S.O. 6 still eating at him? Or was his insistence that Special Ops was the only career that interested him another erroneous stereotype he needed to change?

The humming in the shower stopped just before Tess turned off the water. She'd be stepping out of the tub now, dripping wet, rubbing herself with a towel. In just a few minutes she'd be back here in the living room with him, bringing her smile, her warmth, and her unabashed joy for sex, life, and his company, despite his moods.

She'd made this homecoming far different than what he'd anticipated—and worth every damn minute.

She'd made this summer so perfect he never wanted it to end.

"Hey, Trav?" she called from the bathroom. "Are the T-shirt and sweatpants for me?"

"Yeah," he hollered back. "I didn't want to send you back to your mom's house completely naked. She still thinks I'm a gentleman."

Tess laughed—a sound that rarely failed to make him smile—and Travis went back to finish his message to Clarskie.

Hey, just between us, I've got a question for the old married guy. How did you know the Beckster was the one? You know, different from those other girls we used to pick?

Just wondering, of course. In case I meet someone

and get involved. I wouldn't want to let a good thing go just because I didn't recognize it, right?

Keep your head down and watch your back or I'll be over there personally to kick your ass. You've got such a great lady to come home to, I'd hate to have you screw up the reunion.

See you soon.

Action Man

Travis sent the message and tucked the laptop under the couch before Tess strolled around the corner from the hallway, cinching the drawstring on his sweats so that they wouldn't fall any farther than where they caught, low on her hips. She already had the legs rolled up. The sleeves of his paint-stained USMC T-shirt hung past her elbows. His baggy clothes should have masked everything and made him think of comfort and sleep instead of T and A, but even a glimpse of her belly button as she adjusted the pants seemed to stimulate the blood flowing inside him.

Or was that the feeling he was going to get every time he saw her from this night on—no matter what her state of dress or undress?

In one fluid movement, she dropped the hem of the shirt past her thighs, grabbed a couple of gingersnaps from their late-night nosh and curled up on the couch beside him. That sense of excitement didn't abate.

Clarksie, I'm in deep.

"I, for one, am glad you're not a gentleman all the time." Tess took a healthy bite and leaned back with a tired sigh. "Is it still raining out there?"

Travis curled his arm around her shoulders and offered himself as a leaning post for some quiet talking and warm snuggling. He glanced out the two narrow windows on either side of the front door. "Yeah, it's still coming down. I don't hear the thunder anymore, so I imagine the worst has passed us by. But we'll have some flash flooding by morning."

"What about your dad? Are you still worried about him?"

"A little," he confessed. "He said they'd be safe on the island another night, and he's been dealing with storms worse than this his entire life—"

"—but he's your dad and you love him."

"Yeah." He hugged her even closer and discovered he could still enjoy companionable silence with his best bud.

She bit into the second cookie before speaking again. "I was young when Dad died, but I think what you're feeling must be pretty similar to what Mom went through whenever he was shipped out on assignment. Even in the Quartermaster Corps, he went to some dangerous parts of the world sometimes. She worried about him when he was gone because she loved him and didn't want to lose him. But she had to trust his skills and experience. Trust that the Corps had trained him well and that he and his comrades could handle themselves in any given situation. She could say her prayers and hope for the best, but ultimately, she knew it was out of her hands."

Travis had heard similar stories from his own mother.

Tess went on. "It's normal to worry. But you have to trust that your dad knows what he's doing. He won't take any unnecessary risks that will endanger him or his crew. He'll do his damnedest to survive because…," she linked her fingers through his at her shoulder and offered a comforting squeeze, "he loves you, too. And he wants to come home, just as much as you want him back in one piece."

He turned and pressed a kiss to her temple, thanking her for knowing what to say and that he needed to hear it. She'd shared a truth that every soldier needed to hear. "How come you're so smart?" he teased.

"Well, while I was waiting for you all these years to come home and indulge a few fantasies, I had time to develop some other skills."

"I happen to think you're a very well-rounded woman, Miss Bartlett." He lingered where he was and nibbled on her ear. "A few fantasies, huh?"

"Travis. You've worn me out." Her beautiful blush took away the sting of any scolding. She pushed his chin away and offered him the last bite of her cookie, and he gladly dipped his head to eat the sweet, spicy treat. She smelled like a treat herself. Her freshly washed skin radiated her own personal scent, and the smell of his masculine shampoo on her damp hair made him feel like he'd put his stamp on her all over again

"C'mon," he urged her, stealing a kiss from her lips and turning her in his arms. "You're in better physical shape than any woman I know. Besides," he fell back onto the cushions, dragging her with him so she lay across his chest, "what a way to go."

He stopped up her answering laugh with a kiss and felt her relax on top of him.

A loud, deep thump from outside startled him from his fascination with her bottom lip. Travis turned his face to the side and strained his ears to identify the sound. "Did you hear that?"

"That's the sound of me trying to stifle a yawn." She

pressed a kiss to his exposed neck. "Believe me, I'm willing, but the body—"

"No. That's not it." He did a sit-up, spilling her onto his lap. He wasn't losing it. He'd heard something besides the storm outside.

"Trav?" Now he'd transmitted his alarm to her. He felt it in the way her fingers dug into his shoulders. "Another ghost?"

"No." The enemy.

The screech of tires spinning to find traction on wet pavement was unmistakable.

"I heard *that*," she said, scrambling off him as he pushed to his feet and dashed to the front door.

He paused a moment to spy through the windows, ensuring whatever danger he'd sensed wasn't just outside his door. "Stay put," he ordered. "Leave the lights off."

Seconds later, he swung the door open and snuck out into the moonless canopy of rain. The sound of a well-tuned muscle car being pushed through its gears diverted his attention to the west. Travis ran down the front sidewalk in time to catch a pair of red taillights spinning around the corner and disappearing into the night, heading toward the heart of downtown Ashton. He had no chance to get a license plate or even the make of the car. "Damn."

Their private road didn't get much traffic during rush hour, much less at three in the morning. And no one cruised through at that speed unless they were drunk or being chased by the cops. Or avoiding detection.

He glanced behind him down the road and peered into the darkness around him, finding no signs of burglary or vandalism or an accident. The road was deserted. Not one house had its lights on.

If he hadn't sensed someone watching him or Tess the other night at the concession stand, he might have written the speeding car off as some teens out for a joyride, or a drunk driver. But there *had* been someone watching. He felt that same threat creeping along his spine now, just as surely as he felt the chilling rivulets of rain on his face and shoulders.

Slapping through puddles in his bare feet, Travis hurried back to the house to find Tess huddled just inside the front door. He slipped the dead bolt and gave her a reassuring squeeze before hurrying down the hall to dig up shoes and a shirt and dress in double time.

Tess followed him to the guest room and hovered in the doorway, hugging her arms around her waist. "You're freaking me out a little, Trav. What's going on? Did you see somebody?"

He tied the second shoe before going to her and rubbing his hands up and down her arms. But he had to keep moving before the rain washed away any more clues.

"Bring me a flashlight." He swatted her rear and scooted her down the hall ahead of him. "Kitchen. Top drawer to the left of the sink."

Like a dutiful soldier, she went. But she wasn't so co-operative about staying put inside the house when he went back out to the street to investigate.

"I said to stay—"

"I'm staying with you, thank you very much." She laced her fingers through his and held on. "If someone's prowling around the house and spying on us, I'll feel safer with you than on my own."

Safer with *him*? Hell. He dug down deep and found what was left of the hero inside him. He might not be functioning at one hundred percent of the soldier he once was, but he'd use every bit of what he did have left to keep this special woman safe.

"All right." He turned his hand and latched onto her with a more secure grip. "But if I tell you to run or hit the deck, you do it the instant I say it. Got it?"

"Yes, sir."

Why didn't he believe that?

Because as soon as he turned on the flashlight, she asked, "What are we looking for?"

We. Like a team. Like she intended to conduct her own search, no matter what safety advice he gave her.

"Anything that'll give us a clue to the make of his car. Or tell us if he actually got out and stood."

"Like the popcorn we found the other night."

"Exactly." She pulled away to search the street and sidewalks alongside him. "Stay close," he warned.

"You, too."

Though the rain and night made searching difficult, it didn't take Travis long to locate a tire track, ground into the mud on the opposite side of the street. As the track filled with water, he knelt down and measured off the length and width of it with his hand.

Tess braced her hand on his arm and looked over his shoulder. "Can you tell what kind of car it was by that?"

"Not exactly. But it was small. Something sporty. Judging by the depth of the track, it had a heavy engine."

"Travis, look." He trained the light to the muddy spot where she was pointing. "Footprints."

Half of one, at any rate, that was clear enough to identify a lug sole. Other prints had been driven over and tromped on and obscured by the rain.

"Maybe someone had a flat tire and stopped here to change it," she suggested.

Travis shook his head. "The prints don't line up with the where the car was parked for that to be the case."

He studied the footprints again. Standing on the pavement, he turned himself in the direction of the print. If more lights were on, he'd be getting a clear gander inside the living room to his father's couch. As it was, he could still make out the shadowy shape of the furniture where he and Tess had been intimate. Twice. *Sick.* "No way."

"What?" Tess clutched at his sleeve, trying to understand what he was still piecing together himself.

Though the individual prints weren't clear, the majority of the shapes squished into the mud pointed in the same direction. Dread knotted his stomach as Travis aligned himself with the prints and raised his flashlight to find out what else their three a.m. visitor had been watching.

He muttered a curse and thanked the fates in a silent prayer. Tess's bedroom window was hidden from this angle. But he had a clear view of the Bartlett's front porch and the dark window of the room where Amy slept. He wrapped an arm around Tess's shoulders and tucked her to his side.

"Trav?" She gripped the front of his shirt in a fist that was tight enough to reveal her trembling. "Did I say this whole invisible spy thing was freaking me out?"

He hated thinking what he was thinking. After all these years… "Describe the man you said was asking about me."

"He said he was a friend."

"What did he look like?"

"A little shorter than you. Black hair. Blue eyes. Military."

Damn. Double damn. Triple damn.

Travis pulled Tess into step beside him. "You said you're freaked out, right? Can you handle it if I freak you out a bit more?"

"I don't know. What are you going to do?"

"I'm going to go wake up your sister."

12

"MRS. B, YOU ALWAYS could fix a dynamite cup of coffee."

Maggie Bartlett blushed under Travis's praise. "Thank you, dear. Are you sure all the doors and windows are locked?"

"Yes, ma'am, I checked."

"I'll rest easy, then." Maggie nodded toward the family room. "Now you two run along."

Tess kept her butt firmly glued to the kitchen chair as Travis saluted her mother with a steaming mug and then turned to follow Amy into the family room where they pulled the folding door shut behind them. She focused on the rich brown coffee she cradled between her hands. The clear, dark color reminded her of Amy's eyes, and how they'd gone wide, then shuttered the instant Travis had mentioned that they needed to talk. *About that night.*

It was as if this mystery conversation had been inevitable. They shared a secret. They'd shared a night! Her sister—the pretty one—and Tess's lover had a history.

Suddenly, Tess felt like second choice all over again.

She'd just shared an incredible night with Travis, one that had irrevocably changed how she perceived herself as a sexual being. One that would stay in her memory forever. She'd spent an amazing few days with him, talking and learning and dropping the self-imposed barriers she'd lived with for so long.

And now, after tonight, every moment spent with Travis would be a risk.

To her heart.

Because she loved him.

She'd always loved him. From the first time he'd tossed a ball into her yard and asked her to play, she'd known Travis Harold McCormick was someone she could care about. After that ill-timed encounter in college, she'd never aspired to anything more than the friendship she treasured.

But these last few days together—because he needed her, because she needed him—she no longer just loved him, she'd fallen *in* love.

The depth of what she felt for Travis—made abundantly clear by the twinge of jealousy she was feeling toward her own sister—made the whole idea of walking away from this affair a painful prospect.

Travis and Amy needed to talk *about that night*.

Had they been lovers before Tess had come along?

And what the hell did some creepy bastard who liked to spy on them have to do with it all?

"Should I ask about the outfit?" Maggie pulled out a chair and sat beside her, gently laying her hand over Tess's.

For all of about two seconds, Tess considered telling her mother the truth—that she had an untapped wild side, that she'd snuck out to meet Travis, that she'd fallen in love with him, that she was going to get her heart crushed like a bug on a sidewalk when he left. But her mother had other things to worry about right now, like the sound of Amy's tears coming through the louvered door. Or Travis's calm announcement moments ago that he was sure someone had been outside, casing the house and its occupants, and could they please keep everything locked up tight and follow some basic rules of personal safety until he could double-check a few things, notify the police and get the situation resolved?

Instead, Tess shared a version of the truth. "I was outside in the rain tonight, and Trav lent me some dry clothes."

"So I shouldn't ask why you snuck out of the house just after midnight, either?"

"Mom!"

Maggie waved aside Tess's startled gaze. "I've always been able to tell when one of my girls was out after curfew. Just because you have lives of your own now doesn't mean I've forgotten how to be a mother."

"Curfew?"

"Oh, I know you're only here for a couple of weeks, and that you're grown women and I can't tell you what to do. I just wanted you to know that I think it's about time you *did* start sneaking out."

"Mo-ther."

Maggie leaned in to whisper. "I always wondered when you and Travis would get your heads around the idea that you two aren't children anymore."

They certainly hadn't acted like children tonight. Tess got up and paced to the stove to top up the coffee she'd barely touched. "Travis is leaving Ashton soon, Mom. There's nothing going on."

"Uh-huh." The sound of skepticism wafted across the

kitchen. "He cares about you, Tessa, and you care about him. Be bold. Forget about whatever rules you've set for each other or for yourself. If there's half a chance, don't let happiness get away."

Tess tried and failed to form a smile. "Do I want relationship advice from my mother?"

"My dearest darling, I speak from experience." Maggie crossed the kitchen and wrapped her up in a hug. "Loving a military man isn't an easy thing. There are times when he's gone for months and the loneliness just about eats you up inside. You worry whether or not he's safe or fed or sheltered. Sometimes, he comes home and you've gotten so used to doing things on your own that you have to learn how to be a couple all over again. But if you love the right military man, it's all worth it."

Tess gave her mom a final squeeze before pulling away. "I didn't say anything about love, Mom."

"Uh-huh."

Before she had to explain the subtle difference between a love affair and love, Amy burst through the study door. Her splotchy face showed signs of anger, sorrow and fear. But she didn't allow Tess or their mother to utter a word of concern or offer a bit of comfort.

"Men are such…" Amy twirled about the kitchen, spotting her target "…buttheads."

She grabbed the vase of roses, stormed out to the garage and dumped them into the trash. When she returned, she washed and dried her hands, then dabbed her eyes with the damp towel.

"I'm sorry." The tears started to flow again. Tess took a step toward her, but Amy shooed her away. "I'm sorry. I'm going back to bed. If any men call me, tell them I'm not interested. Tell them I'm not here. I don't care what you tell them. Just keep them away from me."

"Amy?" Travis caught her by the arm as she stalked toward the stairs. She jerked away and he put up his hands in apology. "Can I tell her?"

Oh, God. Tell her what?

For an infinite moment, Amy stared up at Travis as though his request made no sense. Then she turned and pointed to Tess. "You know that night we were talking about the other day, back when I was waitressing at The Bounty?"

The night when something had gone terribly wrong. Something that had scared Amy. Something that made marrying Barry Friesen look like a good idea. Tess braced herself to hear the story. "I remember."

Amy's laugh puffed out in a sob. "It's come back to haunt me." She reached for Travis's hand and gave it a squeeze. "You can tell her. Just don't let him hurt her."

"I won't," Travis promised. "I won't let him hurt any of you. I didn't then. I won't now."

Amy nodded without showing much belief in his vow. She said goodnight and dragged her feet up the stairs. Maggie tightened her robe and hurried to follow.

"I'm staying here tonight." It was a statement, not a request. "To keep an eye on things."

As Tess's mouth rounded in protest, Maggie smiled. "Of course, you are." She patted Travis's arm and whispered loudly enough for her daughter to hear. "The biggest bed is in Tess's room. You'll be most comfortable there."

With a thumbs-up sign, she hurried after Amy.

Tess had never felt quite as awkward with Travis as

she did alone in that kitchen at that moment. "So what's the big secret? Did you and Amy…before you and me?"

Travis crossed the kitchen in three long strides and folded his arms around her. Tess tried to hold on to some pride, but his damp clothes only intensified how good he smelled and how much heat he generated and how close they'd gotten earlier that night. And even if he had smelled like a bucket of fish, this was Travis. And there was no place she'd rather be. Her arms snaked around his waist and she snuggled close.

Exhaling a deep breath, Travis pressed a kiss to her temple. "*You* are the only Bartlett who gets my shorts in a twist."

"Yeah, right."

Travis leaned back and tipped her chin to look him in the eye. "Yeah," he emphasized. "Right." He tucked her under his arm and headed for the stairs. "Now, you want to show me to your bedroom? Your mom gave me the okay."

Tess planted her feet. "The secret first. And why did we have to wake Amy up in the middle of the night to make her cry?"

"That wasn't my intention, believe me." Travis sat in a chair and pulled Tess into his lap. "I promised Amy I would never say anything about the night she was nearly raped."

Tess froze, then swallowed hard around the sudden lump in her throat. "Oh, my God."

"About the night I punched a so-called friend's lights out and helped her get to someplace safe. Amy can give you the details if she wants. But the gist of it is—she used to date a guy from my officer training unit."

"The man with the black hair?" Tess guessed.

He nodded. "Kyle Black. He's a good officer. A good Marine. He and I have competed for a lot of things over the years—I'm not proud of all of them. Promotions, assignments, who had the studliest reputation with the ladies."

She could imagine who won that one. Tess absently plucked at Travis's sleeve. "Don't tell me Amy was a casualty of your competition."

"She and Kyle dated for a while. He was pretty serious. More than she was."

Tess's fingers stilled. A sudden chill drained her of warmth from head to toe. "Wait a minute. You mean like creepy serious? Like stand out in the rain and stalk somebody serious?"

Travis's silence gave her her answer. "He didn't handle rejection very well."

"Poor Amy." Guilt replaced the jealousy she'd felt. "How did you get involved?"

"I helped her walk away. It was like lookin' out for my sister. There was a fight. The cops came. Kyle spent the night in jail and got fined for drunk and disorderly. I drove her home. He claims I took her from him. He's been trying to even the score ever since."

"How awful." Winding her arms around his neck, she hugged him tight. "You'll keep her safe now, won't you?" she whispered against the stubble on his neck. "Until the police catch him or he wises up and goes away on his own?"

"Tess." He called to her in a low, rumbly voice that conveyed more meaning than a simple name. When he pushed her away to look into her eyes, his gaze was saying something more, as well. "If Kyle wants payback with me, Amy isn't the woman he'd try to hurt."

SO THIS WAS what it felt like to have a bodyguard.

But did that mean Travis really cared? Or was he just being a good friend and creature of duty?

This afternoon at the concession stand was proving to be much busier than Monday had been. It might be due to the natural influx of tourists that increased with each day of the festival, or it might have more to do with the gorgeous six-foot-two Marine who was working behind the counter with her, serving up drinks and bagging popcorn. Maybe it was her imagination, but it certainly seemed as if she'd had a lot more female customers than in years past.

Travis had held her through the remainder of the night. He'd called the police and arranged for periodic patrols of the neighborhood. He'd called Morty Camden to shadow Amy's activities throughout the day, which basically meant sitting in a car out in front of the house since she refused to have any interaction with males of any ilk for an indefinite length of time.

Travis had even driven Tess to the hospital that morning and gone through a session of physical therapy with her. They'd worked on weights and mobility without venturing anywhere near the massage table.

If Kyle Black tried to send more flowers and pay a visit, Travis intended to be on hand to greet him in person.

"Yo, Tess."

Tess looked up from the tray of nachos she was prepping to find PFC Thibideux smiling through the screen at her. "Hey, there, boys." Her greeting took in his shorter friend at his side, Corporal Jaynes, as well. "You're here early today."

"It's our last night of leave," Thibideux complained. "So we wanted to get an early start."

Travis stood up from behind the display rack and leaned one hip against it in a relaxed pose. "Boys."

"Sir."

"Sir."

Tess rolled her eyes as the two young noncoms snapped to attention. "Travis, they're on vacation. Give it a rest."

"It's called leave, T-bone. And these men are following protocol." But he was grinning by the time he reached the counter. "At ease, gentlemen. What'll you have?"

In the middle of placing orders and taking money, Travis's cell phone rang. Assuring him she could handle the booth on her own for a few minutes, he took the call.

"McCormick."

Tess tried not to eavesdrop, but Travis's suddenly rigid posture and clipped answers were hard to ignore. She confronted his grim expression when he hung up. "Is it Kyle Black?"

"Harbor Master. They lost contact with the Helena II about an hour ago." He pinched his thumb and forefinger together over the bridge of his nose, fighting the combination of too little sleep and too much stress. "I expected Dad to be home by now. I hope to God it's just the radio giving him fits again."

"You need to go," she stated simply. "Go down to the dock. Take the Helena out if you need to. Go find him."

"I'm not leaving you."

Tess pointed to the line forming behind Jaynes and

Thibideux. "There's a big crowd at the festival today—it's not like I'll be alone." She reached for the tie at the back of Travis's carpenter apron and pulled. "You've got one, maybe two, hours of daylight left." She pushed him toward the door. "Go. Find your father."

He planted his feet at the door and turned. "Kyle's smart. He's tricky. This isn't any practical joke he's trying to pull."

"Your dad needs you, Travis."

"Come with me."

"I can't. I might not be saving the planet or defending my country or even the girl next door. But I have responsibilities, too. Yours is to your dad right now." She tried another push. No budging. "You'd better stop by the house and grab his extra bottle of pills, just in case he's lost his. Go. Time's wasting."

"Jaynes. Thibideux."

"Sir."

"Sir."

Even Tess snapped to at that commanding voice. "What are you doing?" she asked.

But her question fell on deaf ears. Travis had already circled outside and was handing down orders to the two off-duty Marines. "You are not to let her out of your sight. Do you understand?" There was no protest, no mention of leave or the fact he wasn't their commanding officer. Captain McCormick spoke, and these young men fell into line. "If she gets in her car and goes home, you go with her. If she takes a coffee break and leaves the stand, you're by her side."

"Yes, sir."

He turned to bark an order at her. "You see Kyle, you

call the cops. And then you get on the phone and call me. I do not want you alone with that man. Understand?"

Tess refused to snap a "yes, sir," but she had no problem throwing her arms around his neck and pressing a quick kiss to his lips. "I understand. Go."

His arms snaked around her waist and he lifted her off the floor, turning a simple peck on the lips into a heartbreaking, soul-stealing kiss. "Be here when I get back," he whispered against her mouth.

"I will." Her feet returned to earth and she bravely pushed him toward the door. "Say hi to Hal for me."

He pointed one last, stern finger at the noncoms. "You watch her."

"Yes, sir."

"DAD?"

A crackle of static was Travis's only answer.

With his wraparound sunglasses as the only shield to block the wind in his face, he kicked the light trawler up another 10 mph and steered around Beamon's Promontory toward the next fishing cove. Longbow Island in the Atlantic was a good four-hour trip by speedboat, and he'd hit nightfall in half that time, rendering him nearly useless in finding his father without a radio contact to guide him. The Coast Guard would prove a more effective rescue team after dark.

Still, Travis knew more about his father's fishing habits and favorite haunts than the Coast Guard. And until that last bit of sun lit the sky, he could trace his father's meandering path through all the inlets and coves of Chesapeake Bay, where the fishing was best. If the Helena II had faulty equipment, his father wouldn't risk open water on the trip home, anyway. He'd find the nearest port and make repairs, and if that wasn't feasible, then he'd limp along home at a safer route closer to shore.

That's where Travis would find his father. He hoped.

"C'mon, Dad." He went through the radio frequencies one more time. "Helena to Helena II. Dad, if you copy this, send up a flare. We're looking for you. We want you home."

He needed to get home. Kyle Black might not have anything in mind beyond watching and waiting and playing the game. But Travis doubted it. He was the injured man down now. Vulnerable to attack. If Black was smart—and the son of a bitch was—he'd target Travis now, while his future role in the Corps was uncertain. While he was home on leave—alone, without family or platoon-mates to back him up. While he was distracted with his father's disappearance.

Kyle claimed that Travis had stolen Amy from him. She'd been more of a status symbol than a girlfriend, a possession rather than a partner. The prettiest girl in Ashton, the one all the men from OTS had wanted that summer. But Kyle had snagged her with his money and charm and handsome face. He'd been the victor.

But when Amy Bartlett had decided that ownership wasn't to her liking, she'd tried to leave. Kyle had gotten verbally and physically abusive that night in the parking lot. Travis had sucker punched him and driven Amy away to a hotel to hide until Kyle had been returned to Quantico. Amy had slept on the bed; Travis had slept on the floor.

And now, ten years later, Kyle was going to finally take from Travis what he perceived Travis had taken from him.

The woman he loved.

Tess.

"C'mon, Dad," he yelled into the radio. "Tess needs me." He switched off the mike and admitted a truth that scared him even more. "I need her."

How was the Action Man going to settle down with one woman? How was he going to make a relationship work with Tess? How could he be the hero she deserved if he couldn't even track down his own father?

Travis slowed the Helena as he entered the next cove. A human-made jetty of boulders and steel helped control tidal washouts of the rocky beach, and also provided a mammoth feeding ground for a variety of fish, making it a popular destination for fishers with time to travel to the remote location.

He bounced over the waves and turned toward shore. The sun was half a red-orange ball just peeking over the horizon behind him. This would be his last stop before he had to call the Harbor Master and notify the Coast Guard.

The first thing he saw was Eileen Ward's long auburn hair, flying loose in the breeze and flapping like a signal banner. She wore a fluorescent orange life vest at the helm of the Helena II. The trawler rode low in the water and plodded at a minimal speed—not a good sign. Then he saw Walter and Millie Craddock, dumping buckets of water over the sides of the ship.

"Dad?" he whispered. No silver-haired man in sight.

"Dad!" Travis shouted, adrenaline firing through his body. He gunned the engine and set the radio on bullhorn mode. "Helena to Helena II. Do you need assistance? Repeat. Do you need assistance?"

"That's my boy!" Travis heard the shout before he

saw his father climbing up from the engine room. "That's my boy!"

The familiar face needed a shave, but the heart seemed fine—and the spirits were far more buoyant than the boat. Travis pulled alongside as the Craddocks and Mrs. Ward exchanged hugs and handshakes with his father.

Hal McCormick's report was brief. "We hit the rocks on Longbow during the storm. Cracked the hull and busted the radio."

General Craddock's report was even briefer. "Get us the hell off this boat."

Travis tossed them a line and helped the ladies cross over to the Helena. "You want me to rig a tow-line, Dad?"

"Nah. I'll anchor it and come back for it with the trailer."

"If we're lucky, it'll sink," was General Craddock's opinion.

Millie pulled him down beside her on a seat in the stern. "Quit complaining, Walter. That was the grandest adventure we've had in years. Personally, I had fun sharing a pup tent with you."

The two kissed and Travis politely looked away to wrap his dad up in a hug once he got him on board. "Good to see you, old man. You had me worried."

"Good to see you, son." Hal patted him on the back and grinned at Eileen when he stepped away. "We're a little worse for wear, but nothing serious. And there was no chance of starving because Eileen here caught so many fish that we threw one back. I tell you that woman's got a knack."

Eileen's answering smile softened her taut features.

Well, whaddaya know? Travis put the boat in gear,

turned on the headlight and bent his head to whisper to his father. "Dad, you sound as if you're lusting after that woman's ability to catch fish."

"I'm lusting after that woman, period," Hal whispered.

"Dad!"

Hal winked a smiling blue eye. "I'm sixty, son. I'm not dead."

Hmm. The stodgy worrywart he loved so well was laughing, flirting, wrapping himself in the same blanket he draped around Eileen's shoulders.

"How are *you* feeling, son?" Hal asked, once he had Eileen settled at his side.

"Good. Strong. I found you, didn't I?"

"That you did."

Travis picked up speed and headed for deeper water.

Funny how a man could change in just a few short days.

And he wasn't talking about his father.

13

"HEY, BOYS. You ready?"

Tess's two bodyguards, so eager to please a superior officer, flanked her on either side as she locked the concession stand and headed for the parking lot. Jaynes and Thibideux had not only given her a sense of security while Travis was gone, but they'd been good company. Once Jaynes had lightened up and Thibideux had gotten a little more serious, they'd volunteered to work beside her in the stand. When they weren't flush with customers, they'd talked about everything from hometowns to cars to future goals and dreams.

But four hours of playing babysitter when Kyle Black was nowhere in sight? "Why don't you go on and see if you can catch the end of the street dance," she suggested as she continued toward her car. "Or have a beer at The Bounty." She pulled a twenty-dollar bill from her jeans. "Here. They're on me."

"Oh, no, ma'am." Thibideux touched her elbow to push her hand back inside her pocket. "The captain said to stick with you, and unless you're having that beer with us, we're goin' wherever you're goin'."

Tess checked her watch for the fifth time in as many minutes. Where was the captain, anyway?

"I'm sure he'll be calling soon, ma'am." Jaynes had the insight to see how worried she was about Travis.

Had Trav gone all the way to Longbow Island? Had he found Hal, or had the search been tabled until daylight returned? Was Hal all right? Had he suffered another heart attack? Were the Craddocks and Eileen all right? And what about Travis? Was his leg holding up? Was he so worried about Kyle Black that he wasn't following all those safety procedures he kept harping to her about?

Tess nodded a reassurance she didn't quite feel. "I'm sure he will. So, are we having that beer?"

Ten minutes later, Tess was at a table at The Bounty, waiting for a pirate wench to bring them three beers. The bar was crowded and smoky. If she didn't feel she owed her makeshift bodyguards a tangible thanks for giving up the last night of their leave for her, then she'd have skipped the skull-jarring level of music and conversation and headed for home and a hot shower.

The least she could do was give her bladder and eardrums a little peace. She slipped the twenty onto the table and pointed over her shoulder toward the ladies' room in the back. "Remember, they're on me. I need to stop at the little girls' room."

Thibideux climbed off his stool. "I'll go with you."

"No, you won't." Old, reliable Tess would have given up the argument and let the young man accompany her. Correction, the old Tess wouldn't have come here in the first place. Though she felt a little like Mrs. Robinson with the two young studs in tow, she wasn't interested in entertaining the troops herself. She spotted a pretty brunette tapping her foot at the bar. Tess pointed her out.

"Why don't you go ask her to dance. If I'm not out in five minutes, then you can storm the john. Okay?"

"Okay. One dance." Thibbs had to practically shout to be heard. "If you're not at the table when the song's done, I'm coming in."

Tess laughed and gave him a tiny shove toward the brunette. "See if she has a sister for the corporal, too."

The quiet of the rustic, tiled bathroom was almost painful as it rushed in on her eardrums. She waited until a young blond woman had exited and the empty spaces beneath each stall told her she was alone. Tess paused a few moments at the mirror to simply breathe and relax. She looked like she'd put in a full day. Tendrils from her ponytail curled loosely around her forehead and cheeks. Her Royals jersey was wrinkled from where she'd tied the carpenter's bag for change around her waist. She had a spot of nacho cheese in the middle of the white *R* on her left breast, and she looked beat.

But as she leaned in closer to inspect the shadows under her eyes, she wasn't thinking about how her work at the hospital and the concession stand had exhausted her. She was thinking of the night before, and how replete and languid and weary she'd been after making love with Travis. How proud and sexy she felt to know he was completely turned on by her.

Tess leaned in closer to the mirror and touched her lower lip. She gently tugged her mouth open, wet the tips of her fingers and traced the rim of her mouth. Was this the image Travis had seen at his window? She trailed her moist fingers down the length of her throat, slowly mesmerizing herself as she felt the same stirrings of electric energy that had pulsed through her last night.

Had he seen her eyelids grow heavy with passion? Her breathing grow shallow with desire?

Would she ever have another night like that in her life if Travis stuck to the deal they'd made and moved on?

He cared. He loved her as a friend. He wanted her as a woman. He'd given her everything she'd asked of him and more. But it wasn't enough. Two weeks and a kiss goodbye would never be enough with Travis.

Curling her exploring fingers into a fist, she dabbed at the tears stinging her eyes. She couldn't be his friend after this. She couldn't want him this much, love him this way, and simply call him friend.

So what was she supposed to—?

A sharp ringing in her purse startled her from her heartbreaking thoughts. She quickly pulled out the phone and flipped it on. Relief surged through her. "Travis?"

"Uh, no." Amy. "Hey, kiddo. Don't you check the number before you answer?"

She didn't need yet another lecture on personal safety. The last of her patience leaked out on a weary sigh. "I'm tired. What do you want?"

"I just wanted to call to give you a heads-up. Kyle Black was here at the house."

Everything inside Tess tensed.

"Are you okay? Is Mom?" Now she could hear the stress tightening Amy's voice. She hugged her purse beneath her arm, and even in the ladies' room, she couldn't keep herself from glancing over her shoulder. "Did he get into the house? Did he hurt anyone?"

"No. Morty yelled at him." It was triumph, not stress, giving her thirty-five-year-old sister's voice an almost giddy quality. "He threatened to call the police.

He said he didn't give a rat's ass what kind of rights Kyle had to park his car there. I could hear him through the front window. Morty said Kyle was terrorizing Mom and me, and that he needed to move his car now. You should have heard all the rights and regulations he rattled off. Morty cussed!"

Morty Camden?

"You know. If he asks me out again, I'm going to say yes. Heck, if he doesn't ask me out, then I'm asking him."

"Amy?"

"Oh, right. The main reason I called was to warn you. When Kyle left here, he headed straight into town. You'd recognize him, right?"

Black hair, blue eyes, handsome face? "The poster boy for the USMC? I'll know him."

After she hung up, Tess raised her gaze to the mirror. Her startled breath rushed out so fast, she couldn't even scream.

Black hair, blue eyes, handsome face—standing right behind her in the mirror.

"Poster boy for the USMC. I'm flattered. Tess Bartlett?" The hand the man extended toward her held a knife. A jagged, wicked-looking thing that was no overture of friendship. "I'm Kyle Black."

"ARE YOU KIDDING ME with this?" Tess left the ladies' room with Kyle Black right behind her, his arm linked through hers, holding her close. He wedged the knife between them, close enough to cut a hole in her jersey and prick her skin. "I know who you are and what you did to Amy. Are you going to beat me up in the parking lot, too?"

"And give your friend McCormick the chance to

play hero all over again? I'm just taking back what he owes me."

They circled the crush on the dance floor and she caught a glimpse of Thibideux's tall head bobbing over the other dancers. She turned to make eye contact, but Kyle breathed a warning against her ear. "Don't even think it. Both your sidekicks are occupied right now. It's just you and me."

The fresh night air, cleansed by last night's rain, should have revived her, but a creeping sense of helplessness began to consume her as he led her farther away from the noisy throng. "Where are we going?"

"My car." His grip on her wrist tightened with a painful pinch as he turned down a dark alley, taking a shortcut to someplace with lights and people, she prayed.

"My car's closer." It was worth a shot.

"Right. And your car has a bag of baseball bats in the backseat. I'm not arming you."

"You went through my car?"

"You really are missing the point, aren't you." Kyle stopped at the darkest part of the alley, beside a trash dumpster, and pushed her up against the wall. The bricks felt cold and slimy against her back. Captain Black felt warm and slimy against her front. "We can do this easy, or we can do this hard." He ran his hand up her thigh as he nuzzled her neck. "I can make this very nice for you."

"That's called rape, you bastard." She slapped at his hand and squirmed to wedge her arms between them. "There is nothing nice—"

"Shut up." He covered her mouth with a rough hand and shoved her head against the bricks. Stars swirled behind her eyes, but she breathed deeply and blinked to keep his icy eyes in focus. "Believe me, this will be your choice," he promised.

Her skull throbbed. Feeling dizzy, her feet stumbled beneath her as he pulled her along beside him. By the time her vision cleared, they'd left the alley and he was half carrying, half dragging her toward a low-slung red sports car.

"No!" Ignoring the threat of the knife, Tess jammed her elbow into Kyle's gut. His grip loosened with a startled "oof" and she started to run.

But she had nowhere to go. Kyle snatched her by the wrist, slung her around and smacked her back against the car. A bolt of pain radiated along her spine, but it was his hips grinding into hers and the knife at her throat that scared her more.

"That wasn't very nice." He cut one button loose. "I thought Ashton was famous for its summer hospitality." Two more buttons popped loose and her jersey gaped open. "Now you're gonna get into the car, and you're going to do what I tell you."

His fingers bruised her arm as he jerked her to one side and opened the door. Tess's foot rolled on something uneven near the curb. Something long and cylindrical. She braced her hands against the door and frame, resisting when he tried to push her down onto the passenger seat. "What do you want from me?"

"Satisfaction." He breathed the word against her ear, trailed the knife blade along her nape. "Captain McCormick needs to come down a peg or two. You're what he wants, so I will take you."

"My sister didn't want you. I don't want you. You can't force me to—"

"You don't understand." Kyle spun her around and backed her against the car frame. This time, he didn't use violence, but he dropped his voice to such an icy, unemotional timbre that it coiled like a snake along each nerve cell, leaving plenty of fear in its wake. "You don't want to mess with me. McCormick is going to lose one way or the other. You can kiss me, nice and real friendly-like. Or I can hold up his assignment to Special Ops. I can arrange for the paperwork to cross my desk and get lost for a very long time. He'll be a desk jockey for the rest of his career—if he doesn't wash out first."

"He'll never leave the Corps."

"It's your choice, Miss Bartlett—the kiss or the job?"

Tess's right heel rolled across the cylinder again. She had to duck her chin to hide her urge to smile.

There was a third option.

Kyle Black's artificially minty breath washed over her as she thought back to that very first night on the beach with Travis. With that impromptu game of stickball, a friendship had been rekindled, a love affair had been born, and a bond of love and loyalty that she would never break had been forged.

"Travis's career means everything to him," Tess whispered. "I won't let you take that from him."

"So it's the kiss. The betrayal." Kyle sounded pleased.

"Just a kiss, right? You won't force me?"

"We'll see how good you are."

Tess slowly raised her head, using every seductive skill Travis had taught her to give her confidence. "I can be very good."

Kyle laughed as he reached inside her jersey to cup

her breast. He slowly closed the distance between them and covered her mouth with his own.

Interesting. Not a single babble. When Travis kissed her, her thoughts scattered. With Kyle, every impulse was clear as a bell.

She concentrated on her right foot, on moving her lips, on sucking Kyle's bottom lip between her own.

And then she bit. Hard.

"Bitch!" Kyle smacked her across the face as he jerked back and pressed a hand to his bleeding mouth.

Concentrating through the ringing concussion of pain, Tess let the momentum of the blow carry her to the ground. She grabbed the pipe beneath her feet and came up swinging.

A hit to the solar plexus. He doubled over with a raspy curse.

"Keep your mouth and hands…" The knife blade flashed. She swung again. "…and threats to yourself!"

"There she is!"

Kyle roared as the knife flew out of his hand and clattered into the gutter.

"Call 9-1-1!"

"I called as soon as I knew she was gone."

Fear-charged adrenaline drove her now. She lifted the pipe to strike again.

"Tess!" A steel band of arms grabbed her from behind, cinching her arms to her body and lifting her off the ground to keep her from swinging the pipe.

She recognized Travis first by scent, then by the husky voice whispering in her ear. "You got him, babe. You got him. It's all right. You can stop."

"She's a menace, McCormick." The furious haze

began to clear. Kyle Black's face swam in front of hers, his lip bleeding, two fingers hanging at an abnormal angle. "You deserve that ugly excuse for—"

"Hey!" Travis's voice barked a threat. "You want me to let her go so she can practice her home-run swing on you again?"

Tess jerked in Travis's arms and Kyle lurched back. But the poor man had no place to go. Jaynes and Thibideux had him pinned. "You keep her away from me," Kyle protested. "She's crazy."

"You're the one who needs help, Black. Kidnapping a woman from the ladies' room?"

The warmth of Travis's body seeped into hers, and Tess's brain finally cleared. "Travis?"

"I've got you, babe. You're safe now. I'm not going anywhere." His hold on her shifted. He pried the pipe from her hand and passed it back to someone standing behind him. She turned her nose into the salty damp scent that clung to his clothes and he pulled her more fully into his embrace. She felt his lips in her hair and Tess didn't know whether to break into tears or let her shaking knees collapse as the last of the adrenaline drained from her system.

Ultimately, she decided to laugh.

"Captain Black?" She knew that voice.

So did Kyle Black. "General Craddock. Sir."

Major ouch.

"When you're done with the police, you and I need to sit down and have a talk. Captain McCormick?"

Travis straightened without releasing her. "Sir?"

"I know you want that Special Ops position. Call me. Your dad has the number."

"Yes, sir. Thank you, sir."

Tess tightened her hold around Travis's waist. He was getting the job. His dream was coming true.

And in a few short days, her dream would end.

Friday, thirteen hundred hours,
Quantico, Virginia

"I STILL DON'T SEE WHY I had to come. I don't even know these people. They're all from your S.O. unit, right?" Tess had made a gallant effort to keep the conversation light and impersonal on the drive from Ashton. But now that she was here, on the bustling military base that Travis called home, her emotions threatened to get the best of her.

"Yeah. C'mon. They're unloading the personnel bus now. Let's go welcome them home." Travis reached for his white hat, or cover, as he'd called it, and put it on as soon as he climbed out of his father's truck.

Of course, the rat had to look particularly handsome today, spiffed up in his summer class-B uniform with his royal slacks, khaki shirt, and enough ribbons on his chest to start his own flag corps. As he circled the truck to open her door, she admired the way his shoulders and chest accommodated the brass buttons and silver captain's bars. His limp was barely detectable in his proud gait. He was all man. All military. All heartbreaker.

She ought to know.

Tess reluctantly climbed out into his world and smoothed the skirt of her white sundress. When he took her hand to hurry across the parking lot to the bleachers and ceremonial drill field, Tess dug in her heels and held her ground.

"Trav—we've already said goodbye, you and me. Last night was beautiful, every moment of it."

He lifted her fingers to his lips and kissed them. "Yeah. Who knew how creative we could get with red wine?"

She could think of dozens of ways she wanted to get creative with Travis. Every one of them would be sweet or funny or mind-blowingly hot. But her time with him was over.

"This is your world, you belong here." She rested her hand against the scar that lined his jaw and gave him such character. "But I need to go back to mine. The summer's winding down. I need a clean break." The umpteenth tear of the day pricked the corner of her eye, but she refused to shed it, just as she'd refused to shed all the others. "I'm trying to be sophisticated and mature about this. We agreed to two weeks, no strings attached. I need to be done."

"Hey." He brushed his thumb across her cheek. Okay, so maybe one had fallen. "Just trust me for a little while longer, T-bone."

Her heart was doomed. She wouldn't have thought a friend could be so cruel.

Travis pulled her into step beside him and they wove their way through the waiting crowd. After a brief ceremony, with music and thank-you's and very short speeches, the men and women in their desert khaki uniforms were unleashed. Tess found herself openly crying at the reunions of husbands and wives, fathers and children, sisters and brothers, parents and sons and daughters. She laughed at noisy toddler kisses and stole Travis's handkerchief when she saw a father meeting his newborn daughter for the first time.

And something stirred, low in her belly and deep in her heart, when she saw quite possibly the largest man she'd ever seen in person pick up a rather Rubenesque-looking blonde and spin her around before dropping to one knee and pulling her onto his lap to claim the woman's mouth in the most passionate of kisses.

"Welcome home, I guess," Tess murmured in admiration and maybe a touch of jealousy. That man and woman were in love.

"They're something, huh?" Travis's arm settled with possessive familiarity around her waist. "Come on. I want you to meet an old friend."

He took her over to the passionate giant and his beaming wife. "Hey, Clarksie!"

"Action Man!"

"Welcome home, buddy." The two men traded handshakes and hugs before introductions were made. "Tess, this is Zachariah Clark. He and I were in Special Ops together for a lot of years."

"This is my wife, Becky."

There were more handshakes and kisses on cheeks, and Clarksie picked Tess right up off the ground before slapping Travis on the back and commenting on his uniform with a grim expression. "I see you're not in Charlie uniform. Does that mean the top brass denied your request to return to S.O. 6?"

What? Travis hadn't said a word. He must be crushed. That explained why he'd wanted the extra company on the trip from Ashton to Quantico.

"Trav, I…" She didn't know what to say.

"I didn't give them the chance." Travis spoke to his big friend, but his blue eyes were glued on Tess. And that grin didn't belong to a man who'd been denied everything he'd always wanted. "I asked to be transferred to the training division. General Craddock approved it yesterday." He glanced at his friend. "I'm going to be teaching the yahoos who are going to take your place one day."

Clarksie shook his head in disbelief and then smiled. "Congratulations, man. What changed your mind?"

"I realized I couldn't give the hundred and ten percent S.O. teams need anymore. But I figure I can eke out about a hundred and one percent to whip some of those new boys into shape." His blue eyes darkened with a double meaning. "I learned I make a pretty good coach."

"I'll bet."

"I get to choose most of my own staff." Travis jabbed Clarksie in the arm. "I could use a big hard-ass like you on the team."

"I'll think about it." Clarksie's gaze—and hands—went back to his wife. The idea of taking an assignment closer to home probably sounded pretty appealing right now.

"Well, you've got a homecoming I'm not going to keep you from. Take care, buddy."

"You, too."

The crowd had pretty much thinned out by the time Tess and Travis got back to his truck. The parking lot was nearly deserted as the returning Marines hurried to get back to their homes and lives for whatever leave they had coming.

When Travis opened the passenger door and lifted her to the seat, Tess held on to his shoulders before he could move away. "Why didn't you tell me about your new assignment?"

His hands settled atop her thighs. "I think I wanted

you to see me in my element, so you could understand that this is something I really want. That I'm not settling for anything."

"Are you really happy with a stateside training assignment?" She smoothed her palms across the crisp, pressed cotton that covered his beautiful chest.

He removed his cover and laid it on the dashboard of the truck. Then he nudged her knees apart and moved in between. His blue eyes never left hers. "Do I look happy?"

She traced her thumb across his smile. "Yes. Congratulations. I'm proud of you."

He slipped his hands beneath her skirt and worked his thumbs along the inside of her thighs. "I've seen my father change from a worried old man to a younger man who's dating again. I saw Morty Camden step it up. And I realized I was trying too hard to keep things from changing, when I really needed to evolve into a better, richer, wiser man."

She tugged on his collar and pulled him in to give him a kiss. "I love the new you."

He took her sweet kiss and deepened it into something spicy. "I love you, too."

For several minutes, they clung to each other, kissing and tonguing and thoroughly exploring each other's mouths. Tess scooted as close as she could to the edge of the seat without falling. Not that he'd let her. She wound her arms around his shoulders and rubbed her perky breasts against his hard, unforgiving body. His thumbs had slid inside her panties to torment her into a panting, babbling wanton.

"Trav...public...see...?" He slipped his thumb between her slick, swelling folds to rub her throbbing nub. She gasped at the shimmers of delicious pleasure arcing to that hidden spot. Her thighs convulsed around his hand, aching to relieve the pressure building inside her.

She'd just about given up trying to talk.

Travis knew his power over her, too. He laughed against her mouth. "Kyle Black got one thing right."

The name nearly broke the spell Travis's hands were weaving beneath her skirt.

"What's that?"

"He knew that *you* were the way to get to me. Losing you is what could hurt me the most. More than any damn bomb or gimp leg or stupid desk job. If I don't have you to make me laugh and make me hot and make me feel like more of a man than I ever hoped to be, then none of it matters."

"You're everything to me too, Travis."

He pulled one hand free to slide the strap of her sundress off her shoulder and then traced the same path with his lips." I know you're pretty attached to Ashton, that you want to be close to your mom and you've got a good job there—but how would you feel about moving a few hours away, say, outside Quantico, Virginia?"

"Why?" He nipped at her collarbone and pressed his warm, moist lips to the swell of her breast above the dress's neckline. "Am I…Corps…joining?"

"Probably not. But I'm hoping you'll give some serious thought to sharing lots of time with one particular Marine."

"What?" Tess pulled herself from the haze of passion to make sure she'd heard that right. She caught his jaw between her palms and lifted his face to meet her gaze.

"What are you saying? Keep in mind that I'm fairly new to all this and that I don't want to misunderstand."

"New? Ha. You're a ringer, you sex goddess." That killer McCormick smile made his message very clear. "I think we can be friends *and* lovers. Have the best of both relationships."

"Don't they call people like that a couple?"

"Sometimes they call them a married couple."

"Hmm." Tess scooted to the middle of the truck's wide bench seat, giving Travis room enough to climb inside with her. "Now that's a role I haven't tried yet."

He closed the door behind him. "I have a feeling you'll be very good at it."

She unhooked his brass buckle and reached for his zipper. "I think *we'll* be very good at it. Like a few other things we've tried. Can your knee handle this position?" she asked before untucking the hem of his shirt.

His knee was much better, thank you.

"I think you're trying to wrinkle my uniform, T-bone."

"That's not all I'm trying to do." She lay back on the seat behind the steering wheel and lifted her knees. "Travis?"

He was peeling away her panties and looking his fill of her needy, weeping center. "Tess?"

He wasn't getting it. Yet. She started unbuttoning the front of her dress, inviting the shameless hussy inside her to come out. "Travis."

"Oh." He kissed her breast before gathering her in his arms and sinking between her legs. "I want you, too, Tess. Forever."

DON'T TEMPT ME...
by *Dawn Atkins*

Boudoir photographer Samantha Sawyer's serious new assistant, Rick West, is a little…different. But he *is* good at the job. He's also incredibly hot, which has Samantha wondering what else they could be doing in the boudoir…

AFTERNOON DELIGHT
by *Mia Zachary*

Rei Davis is tough-talking, but wants to show her softer side. Chris London is light-hearted, but wants someone to take him seriously. And when Rei walks into the dating agency Chris owns, the computer determines that they're a perfect match…

THE DOMINO EFFECT
by *Julie Elizabeth Leto*

Domino Black is a spy who has been assigned to seduce Luke Brasco. They begin an affair based on raw sexual energy and lethal lies, but as their emotions start to run deeper, Domino and Luke have to make the decision between life and love.

INNUENDO
by *Crystal Green*

When his insensitive cousin stands up his blind date, good boy Murphy Sullivan offers to pose as bad boy Kyle. But he finds Tamara irresistible – and Murphy can't resist pretending to be his uninhibited cousin – just for a few wild nights…

On sale 4th May 2007

Available at WHSmith, Tesco, ASDA, and all good bookshops
www.millsandboon.co.uk

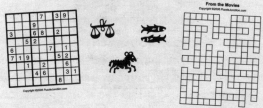

Three utterly romantic, red-hot stories of heroines who travel back in time to meet the one!

What if you had the night of your life...

60 Years Ago?

80 Years Ago?

200 Years Ago?

"The idea of finding your soulmate in the past is romantic and all three contributing authors have done an excellent job providing a little bit of magic in this anthology."
—*Romantic Times*

Available 20th April 2007

www.millsandboon.co.uk

A tale of extraordinary love and passion from *New York Times* bestselling author DIANA PALMER

For anthropologist Phoebe Keller and FBI agent Jeremiah Cortez, the urgent stirrings of mutual attraction are cruelly interrupted when fate – and family loyalties – force them apart.

After three years of anguished separation, the dormant spark of their passion is rekindled when they are reunited by a mysterious phone call about a murder investigation and a robbery of priceless artefacts. But when Phoebe becomes the prime target of a desperate killer, Cortez must race against time to save the only woman he has ever loved.

Available 6th April 2007

2 FREE

BOOKS AND A SURPRISE GIFT!

We would like to take this opportunity to thank you for reading this Mills & Boon® book by offering you the chance to take TWO more specially selected titles from the Blaze™ series absolutely FREE! We're also making this offer to introduce you to the benefits of the Mills & Boon® Reader Service™—

- ★ FREE home delivery
- ★ FREE gifts and competitions
- ★ FREE monthly Newsletter
- ★ Exclusive Reader Service offers
- ★ Books available before they're in the shops

Accepting these FREE books and gift places you under no obligation to buy, you may cancel at any time, even after receiving your free shipment. Simply complete your details below and return the entire page to the address below. You don't even need a stamp!

YES! Please send me 2 free Blaze books and a surprise gift. I understand that unless you hear from me, I will receive 4 superb new titles every month for just £3.10 each, postage and packing free. I am under no obligation to purchase any books and may cancel my subscription at any time. The free books and gift will be mine to keep in any case.

K7ZED

Ms/Mrs/Miss/Mr ....Initials ....

BLOCK CAPITALS PLEASE

Surname ....

Address ....

....

...................................Postcode...................................

Send this whole page to:
UK: FREEPOST CN81, Croydon, CR9 3WZ